GILBERT WITHOUT SULLIVAN

Stories by

W.S. GILBERT

Dramatised for radio by

STEPHEN WYATT

Copyright Stephen Wyatt 2008
All rights are reserved.
Any enquiries regarding performance or reproduction
should be addressed to the author's agents, Valerie Hoskins
Associates, 20 Charlotte Street, London W1P IHJ
Telephone (020) 76374490

ISBN 978-0-9556868-2-5

CONTENTS

PREFACE	5
THE FINGER OF FATE	7
AN ELIXIR OF LOVE	39
THE BURGLAR'S STORY	77
WIDE AWAKE	117
MR. FOSTER'S GOOD FAIRY	157
A SENSATION NOVEL	195

PREFACE

The first five plays are based on stories collected by W.S. Gilbert himself in Foggerty's Fairy and other tales published in 1890.

The Finger of Fate was first published in Routledge's Annual for 1890.

An Elixir of Love published in The Graphic Christmas Number for 1869 is, of course, the inspiration for Gilbert and Sullivan's first full length comic opera, The Sorcerer, first produced in 1877.

This radio version of The Burglar's Tale, first published in Routledge's Annual for 1890, was the starting point for The Burglar's Opera written by Jeff Clarke and Stephen Wyatt. The Opera della Luna production premiered in Chipping Norton in 2004 and toured nationally in 2005.

Wide Awake was first published in Mirth in 1878.

Mr. Foster's Good Fairy is based on Foggerty's Fairy, published in Temple Bar in 1880. Gilbert dramatised the story himself in a version which premiered at the Savoy in 1881. The reason for the name change here is that I had already appropriated the name of Foggerty for the originally anonymous anti-hero of The Finger of Fate.

A Sensation Novel has its origins unlike the others in one of Gilbert's early stage works, first performed at the Gallery of Illustration in 1871. The original text can be found in Gilbert Before Sullivan edited by Jane W. Stedman and first published in 1967.

The scripts were all commissioned and produced by the B.B.C. and first heard on Radio 4.

SJW

THE FINGER OF FATE

First broadcast on Radio 4 on 25th December 2002 with the following cast –

GILBERT	Jonathan Coy
FOGGERTY	Stephen Moore
DOLLY	Alison Steadman

Others parts were played by Martin Hyder and Ian Masters.

The director was SALLY AVENS

	(GILBERT'S VOICE HEARD MUTTERING IN AN UNDERTONE:)
GILBERT:	Well, you get some repose in the form of a doze, with hot eyeballs and head ever aching, But your slumbering teems with such horrible dreams that you'd very much better be waking –
	(A BRIGHT BLAST OF ONE OF SULLIVAN'S OVERTURES) (GILBERT COUGHS. IT CUTS OFF)
GILBERT:	(V.O.) Ahem – Gilbert <u>without</u> Sullivan.
	(ANOTHER BLAST OF SULLIVAN – AGAIN CUT OFF)
GILBERT:	(V.O.) I said – <u>without</u> Sullivan. (CLEARS THROAT) Ahem. The Finger of Fate. An original tale by W.S.Gilbert – <u>without</u> the collaboration of Sir Arthur Sullivan. (EXPECTANT PAUSE. SILENCE.) Thank you. Today I am going to give you an instance of the desperately strong measures Fate will take in order to bring about an event she has set her mind on.
	(THE SOUND OF CONTENTED SNORING)

GILBERT:	(V.O.) Mr. Frederick Foggerty was a middle-aged bachelor, of staid and careful habits. He was pretty comfortably off, having an independent income of £400 a year and a Civil Service pension of £700 a year.
FOGGERTY:	(CHILDLIKE IN HIS SLEEP) Hush-a-bye, baby, on the tree top…
GILBERT:	(V.O.) He was also for many years Secretary of the Warrant Officers' Shirt-frill and Shaving-soap department, a branch office under the Admiralty, Somerset House.

(CROSSFADE TO A CLOCK TICKING. THREE MEN QUIETLY DOZING)

GILBERT:	(V.O.) Mr Foggerty led a quiet and retired life.
FIRST FRIEND:	(YAWNING) Is that really the time? Well, well!
SECOND FRIEND:	(YAWNING) Doesn't the time fly, eh?
FOGGERTY:	(YAWNING) Soon be time for bed.
GILBERT:	(V.O.) He shunned society and associated intimately with the other heads of subordinate departments – but no one else.
FIRST FRIEND:	(YAWNING) It's been a most entertaining evening, Foggerty.
SECOND FRIEND:	(YAWNING) Pity it has to end.
FOGGERTY:	But then – time flies!

	(A LOUD YAWN IN TRIPLICATE) (RETURN OF CONTENTED SNORING)
FOGGERTY:	(SINGING IN HIS SLEEP) Take a pair of sparkling eyes…
GILBERT:	(V.O.) (CROSSLY) I said – without Sullivan. Anyway, Mr Foggerty was a naturally nervous individual.
FEMALE FRIEND:	My dear Mr Foggerty, how lovely to see you, I'd been hoping that you'd come and see my dear little baby with his adorable new outfit – all in red and yellow -
FOGGERTY:	(IN PAIN) Arrrgh!!!
GILBERT:	(V.O.) He hated bright colours –
FEMALE FRIEND:	I do so hope you can if the weather holds out. You never know do you whether it's going to rain or shine. Well, that's the English weather for you, isn't it, and –
FOGGERTY:	(IN PAIN) Ohhhh!!!
GILBERT:	(V.O.) He hated unnecessary conversation –
SINGER:	(PASSING BY) A wandering minstrel, I, a thing of shreds and patches…
GILBERT:	(V.O.) He particularly hated useless noises – such as vocal music –
	(ANOTHER SNATCH OF A SULLIVAN OVERTURE)
GILBERT:	(V.O.) And instrumental music.

	(THE NEIGHING OF HORSES)
FOGGERTY:	(IN PAIN) Ooooohhh!
GILBERT:	(V.O.) He hated the neighing of horses –
	(THE MARCHING OF TROOPS VERY FAST)
OFFICER:	(VERY FAST) Left, right, left, right, left, right, left, right, left –
FOGGERTY:	(IN PAIN) Eeeeeekkkk!!!
GILBERT:	(V.O.) And he couldn't bear to see people in quick motion.
	(THE RATTLE OF A HORSE-DRAWN OMNIBUS)
GILBERT:	(V.O.) But above all other things, he detested forward people –
MAN:	(IN OMNIBUS) Excuse me, sir –
FOGGERTY:	No –
MAN:	I just wondered if you could tell me the way to –
FOGGERTY:	(IN PANIC) I can't tell you anything!
MAN:	Look, all I need to know is whether the next stop is the stop for –
FOGGERTY:	I can't! I can't!
	(HE RINGS THE OMNIBUS BELL)
FOGGERTY:	Let me off, I say! Let me off!

GILBERT:	(V.O.) And, above all other forward people, he detested strangers who addressed him on immaterial topics in public conveyances.
	(CROSSFADE TO THE YAWNING FRIENDS)
FIRST FRIEND:	(YAWNING) Who'd have thought it?
SECOND FRIEND:	(YAWNING) How time flies!
GILBERT:	(V.O.) But in the end retirement loomed. Mr Foggerty was sadly missed by his colleagues.
FIRST FRIEND:	(YAWNING) It's the end of an era!
SECOND FRIEND:	(YAWNING) Nothing will ever be the same.
BOTH:	(YAWNING) How will we ever manage without you?
GILBERT:	(V.O.) So Mr Foggerty was free to fulfil his dream of –
FOGGERTY:	(DREAMING) Peace, perfect peace.
GILBERT:	(V.O.) And here is where Mr Frederick Foggerty made a fatal mistake. He dreamed of a beautiful sunny island –
	(ISLAND MUSIC. THE DESERT ISLAND DISCS THEME?)
FOGGERTY:	(ENCHANTED) Ahhhhh!!!!
GILBERT:	(V.O.) And in that moment he resolved to visit the West Indies. The West Indies, he had heard, were picturesque and idyllic and

	tranquil. There he would find the peace that so often eluded him in the bustle of London. So the finger of fate picked him out – and - another bad mistake – he decided to travel by rail to Liverpool to catch a boat to Jamaica. He did this, reluctantly, fearing the kindness of strangers, but in search of ultimate peace-
FOGGERTY:	(THOUGHTFULLY) It is undoubtedly true that a railway journey to Liverpool is detestable. But there is no other route to Jamaica and – unfortunately - walking there is out of the question.
	(THE SOUNDS OF A BUSY RAILWAY STATION)
FOGGERTY:	Excuse me, guard –
GUARD:	Yes, sir?
FOGGERTY:	This is the train to Liverpool?
GUARD:	Yes, sir. Unless I'm much mistaken.
FOGGERTY:	But there are only four first-class carriages –
GUARD:	That many?
FOGGERTY:	But – they're occupied by…women.
GUARD:	I'm sorry, sir.
FOGGERTY:	One in each carriage. (PAUSE) Apart from the smoking carriage, that is.
GUARD:	I'm not quite with you, sir. Are women a problem?

FOGGERTY: No, no, no. (PAUSE) But people are.
GUARD: So you want to get into the smoking compartment?
FOGGERTY: Yes. Even though I don't smoke.
GUARD: You're a sad case, aren't you, sir?
FOGGERTY: If you say so, guard. But –
GUARD: Listen, sir, just get into the smoking compartment. It's very unlikely we'll take up any first-class passengers on our way.
FOGGERTY: But can you guarantee me that –
GUARD: Sir, without wishing to press you to make a decision – the train is about to depart.

(THE SOUND OF A WHISTLE)

FOGGERTY: Yes, but –
GUARD: (FIRMLY) Sir – get in.

(CUT TO THE RATTLE OF A TRAIN IN MOTION)

GILBERT: (V.O.) So Mr Foggerty got in. The train started and he had the carriage all to himself. In fact, the train didn't stop until they reached Rugby.

(OPENING OF THE CARRIAGE DOOR.

DOLLY: (DEEP VOICE) This is the Liverpool train, isn't it?

GILBERT:	(V.O.) At Rugby a lady opened the carriage door. She was a determined-looking middle-aged woman of decidedly ample proportions dressed in showy colours. Fate's digit was at work again.
FOGGERTY:	I beg your pardon, ma'am, but this is a smoking compartment.
DOLLY:	I can see that. But it so happens that I smoke. Do you have a light by any chance?
FOGGERTY:	(AT A LOSS) Well, I er – well, no, actually I don't.
GILBERT:	(V.O.) This, something told Mr Foggerty, was no ordinary lady.
DOLLY:	Oh well, no consequence. (VERY LOUD:) Guard!!!
GUARD:	(HURRYING UP) Yes, ma'am?
DOLLY:	Can you give me a light for my cigar?
GUARD:	Of course, ma'am. (CALLING) Mind the doors, please.

(THE CARRIAGE DOOR IS SLAMMED. THE TRAIN STARTS UP. A CONTENTED SIGH FROM DOLLY)

DOLLY:	Ahhhh…

(QUIETLY AT FIRST BUT THEN WITH INCREASING VOLUME AND FREQUENCY, FOGGERTY STARTS TO COUGH. OVER THIS:)

GILBERT:	(V.O.) The fumes from the stout lady's Havana cigar filled the compartment. Eventually Mr Foggerty could stand it no more.
FOGGERTY:	I beg your pardon, ma'am, but I'm afraid I object to smoking.
DOLLY:	(PUFFING AWAY) I beg your pardon, sir, but if you object to smoking, why are you travelling in a smoking carriage?
FOGGERTY:	Well, I –
DOLLY:	It don't seem very logical.
FOGGERTY:	I – I entered this carriage to avoid the society of ladies.
DOLLY:	Me too.
FOGGERTY:	But surely –
DOLLY:	I hate the company of ladies too. I prefer gentlemen.
FOGGERTY	Really, madam, I –
DOLLY:	Even you. You're a difficult old customer but I like you, you funny old stick.
FOGGERTY:	Madam, I am not a funny old stick.
	(FOGGERTY GIVES A SNORT OF INDIGNATION. THE TRAIN RATTLES ON.)
GILBERT:	(V.O.) Mr Foggerty sat in affronted silence amid the fug of cigar smoke. Then he hit upon a way to retaliate. He let down a window.
	(SOUND OF CARRIAGE WINDOW BEING LET DOWN)

FOGGERTY: (DEFIANTLY) There, that's better.

DOLLY: I agree. I love fresh air. Shall I let this one down too?

(SOUND OF CARRIAGE WINDOW BEING LET DOWN)
(A HOWLING GALE FILLS THE CARRIAGE)

FOGGERTY: (SNEEZING) Achooo! Oh this is impossible. It's freezing.

(SOUND OF CARRIAGE WINDOW BEING PUT UP.)

DOLLY: Good idea.

(SOUND OF CARRIAGE WINDOW BEING PUT UP)
(THE GALE CEASES)
(A WINDOW LET DOWN. ANOTHER WINDOW LET DOWN. THE GALE RETURNS.)
(A WINDOW PUT UP. ANOTHER WINDOW PUT UP. GALE CEASES.)
(AD. LIB AT INCREASING SPEEDS UNTIL NO LONGER FUNNY. THEN:)

GILBERT: (V.O.) By this time Mr Foggerty was sulkily furious. But in half an hour the train would reach Stafford and then he would be able to change compartments. In the meantime he tried to sleep.

DOLLY:	(CHATTILY) So where are you off to, you stuffy old passenger. Secret, is it? Nothing to be ashamed of, I hope. (PAUSE) I know, you're a trusted cashier bolting with the takings from the bank! (PAUSE) No? Then perhaps you're a confidential clerk with your employer's cash box in your portmanteau? Eh?
FOGGERTY:	(STIFFLY) Madam, I am trying to sleep.
DOLLY:	(OBLIVIOUS) Oh I know! You're an old boy going up north to marry some old girl on the sly, eh?
FOGGERTY:	Madam, please-
DOLLY:	It's all right, nothing shocks me, lovey.
FOGGERTY:	(AGHAST) Lovey!!!
	(PAUSE. THE TRAIN RATTLES ON.)
DOLLY:	So have a guess now - what do you think I am?
FOGGERTY:	I've no idea.
DOLLY:	So you don't think I'm a Duchess then? No! Or a Countess? No! Or a lady of large property – wife of a Liverpool merchant? Course not. Missionary maybe? Nah! Tightrope walker? Not with my figure. So how about the stewardess on a steamship, spending up her pay? So what do you say to that idea, you funny old -

	(A SUDDEN SNAPPING SOUND)
FOGGERTY:	What's that?
GILBERT:	(V.O.) The carriage suddenly slackened speed and eventually stopped. Mr Foggerty put up the window and looked out.
	(SOUND OF WINDOW BEING PUT UP AGAIN)
FOGGERTY:	(IN HORROR) Good heavens!
DOLLY:	(CALMLY) What's happened?
FOGGERTY:	The coupling has broken. The train's left us behind. (PANICKING) The driver knows nothing about it and here we are, halfway between Rugby and Stafford at 12 p.m. on a very cold April night! And it's started to pour with rain!
DOLLY:	Calm down, you silly old fusspot. The Guard's at the end of the train. If we've broken off, he's broken off too.
	(SOUNDS IN DISTANCE OF RUNNING FOOTSTEPS)
GILBERT:	(V.O.) And indeed the guard now rushed past, moving his lantern in the faint hope of being able to attract the attention of the driver. But in vain.
	(FOOTSTEPS RETURNING AT WALKING PACE)

FOGGERTY:	Guard! Guard!
GUARD:	(FROM OUTSIDE, GLUMLY:) Yes, sir?
FOGGERTY:	What in the world are we to do?
GUARD:	Well, I think you'd better get out of this, sir, you and your old woman –
FOGGERTY:	But she is not my old woman -
GUARD:	Suit yourself, sir. But I'm going to run back to Tamworth to telegraph. But it's safest if you and your old woman –
FOGGERTY:	She is not –
GUARD:	Whatever you say, sir, but I'd get out if I were you.
FOGGERTY:	But where are we to go? It's raining hard and we shall be soaked through and through.
GUARD:	There's a light yonder across the common. You better trot over there, you and your old woman, or whatever you choose to call her. I don't know the country just here.
FOGGERTY:	But-
GUARD:	(DISAPPEARING) Good luck, sir!
	(FEET RUNNING OFF INTO DISTANCE.)
FOGGERTY:	So what do we do now?
DOLLY:	The guard's talking sense. I take your arm and off we trot.
FOGGERTY:	(AGHAST) But – I hardly know you.

DOLLY:	That's easily remedied. I'm Dolly - Dolly Fortescue. And you?
FOGGERTY:	(MISERABLY) Frederick Foggerty.
DOLLY:	Looks like Fate's brought us together, eh?
FOGGERTY:	(GLUMLY) Yes.
DOLLY:	Well, then, out into the night we go, Frederick! Our big adventure begins!

(CROSSFADE TO POURING RAIN, CLAPS OF THUNDER, FEET TRUDGING THROUGH MUD.)

GILBERT:	(V.O.) They had a squashy walk over a pathless and furzy common.

(A SUDDEN SQUEAL FROM DOLLY, FOLLOWED BY COLLAPSE INTO THE MUD)

GILBERT:	(V.O.) Unfortunately, Mr Foggerty's companion had a knack of tumbling down in a sitting attitude at the faintest provocation.
DOLLY:	(WINSOMELY) Oh dear, there I go again. (PAUSE) Mr Foggerty Frederick
FOGGERTY:	(GRITTED TEETH) Very well.

(MUCH STRAINING AND PUFFING AS DOLLY IS PULLED BACK UPRIGHT)

GILBERT:	(V.O.) If Mr Foggerty lifted her once, he lifted her twenty times.
	(ANOTHER SQUEAL AND ANOTHER COLLAPSE)
DOLLY:	Coo-ee! Mr Foggerty!
GILBERT:	(V.O.) Panic was rising in his soul. If he helped this woman of some sixteen stone get up twenty times, he would have lifted some two tons in the course of one evening.
DOLLY:	Mr Foggerty !
FOGGERTY:	He had this overwhelming feeling that if he did not move now he would then be trapped into spending the night with this woman.
DOLLY:	Can you hear me, Mr Foggerty?
GILBERT:	(V.O.) Finally – he made his decision.
	(FOOTSTEPS START TO RUN THROUGH THE MUD)
DOLLY:	Mr Foggerty – don't be silly. The light's over there. You're running in the wrong direction. Mr Foggerty!
	(HER VOICE FADES AWAY. THE RUNNING CONTINUES)
GILBERT:	(V.O.) Mr Foggerty did not care where he ran. Just so long as it was away from Dolly Fortescue. Eventually he found a pigsty to lay his weary head – fortunately

currently unoccupied by pigs - and the next morning resumed his journey.

(THE BUSTLE OF A BUSY PORT. A STEAMER'S HOOTER ANNOUNCING DEPARTURE.)

GILBERT: (V.O.) When he finally reached Liverpool, he found that his boat was on the point of sailing. His luggage had been placed on board and his cabin was ready for him.

FOGGERTY: Ahhhh! Peace at last. Jamaica, you blest island of tranquillity, here I come.

GILBERT: (V.O.) Mr Foggerty looks forward to a calm peaceful crossing. (PAUSE) Unfortunately, he looked forward in vain.

(SUDDEN VIOLENT SEA EFFECTS, STORMS, WAVES ETC.)

GILBERT: (V.O.) The weather was unbelievably dreadful and the ship was driven many hundred miles out of its course.

(LURCHING WAVES. CROSSFADE TO WAVES OUTSIDE AND FOGGERTY GROANING WITHIN)

FOGGERTY: Ohhhhh! Ohhhhh! Ohhhh!

GILBERT:	(V.O.) For three weeks after leaving Liverpool, Mr Foggerty was terribly ill…
FOGGERTY:	Ohhhhh! Ohhhhhhhhhh!
GILBERT:	(V.O.) He did not leave his cabin. He could not eat. He could sleep. He could not talk to anyone.
FOGGERTY:	Ohhhhhhhhhh! Ohhhhhhhhhhh!
GILBERT:	(V.O.) Home sweet home had never seemed more alluring. But he might have lain there groaning forever in his cabin but one stormy night –

(DOORS CRASHING OPEN, STORMS, A TERRIBLE CREAKING OF TIMBERS AND LURCHING)

FOGGERTY:	(IN MOTION) Ahhhhh…
GILBERT:	(V.O.) A tremendous concussion threw him bodily out of his cabin. He rushed on deck – and found everything in the wildest confusion.

(COLOSSAL STORM, SHRIEKING PEOPLE)

FOGGERTY:	What's happened?
SAILOR:	The ship's shifted her cargo.
FOGGERTY:	But - what does that mean?
SAILOR:	It means – (SUDDENLY WILD) Abandon ship!

	(OTHER VOICES TAKE UP THE CRY. STORM CONTINUES.)
OTHERS:	Abandon ship! Abandon ship!
GILBERT:	(V.O.) The advice being offered was remarkably clear and simple.
FOGGERTY:	I must abandon ship at once!
	(THE SEA RAGES. PEOPLE CONTINUE TO CRY OUT)
GILBERT:	(V.O.) The vessel was foundering. It was impossible to launch a boat even if it could have survived in such a sea. I don't want to harrow anybody but the prospects were not good. Apart from those of Mr. Foggerty that is.
FOGGERTY:	Oh well, nothing for it.
	(HE STARTS TO BLOW INTO SOMETHING)
GILBERT:	(V.O.) Sometimes it pays to be a bachelor of exceptionally cautious habits. When at sea, Mr Foggerty took the precaution of wearing a little india-rubber apparatus round his neck. It was a nuisance while eating soup but in a crisis like this it really came into its own.
	(THE BLOWING CONTINUES. SHRIEKS AND

	WAILS BEHIND AS PEOPLE JUMP OFF THE BOAT)
GILBERT:	(V.O.) It was a matter of a few moments to inflate it. And then Mr Foggerty was ready to jump!
FOGGERTY:	(SCREWING UP HIS COURAGE) One, two, three – jump! (HE JUMPS.) Ahhhhhhhhhhhhhh!
	(HE LANDS IN THE WATER WITH A LOUD SPLASH. SUDDENLY THE STORM EFFECTS ARE CUT OFF.) (GENTLY LAPPING WATER. SLEEPY LAGOON EFFECTS)
FOGGERTY:	(FLOATING GENTLY) Hush a by, baby…
GILBERT:	(V.O.) After some hours, Mr Foggerty came to. The storm had abated. He was floating gently in the ocean sustained by his trusty india-rubber neck-piece. Really, these devices cannot be recommended too highly. But his troubles were not yet over.
FOGGERTY:	No sign of land… No sign of a sail… No sign of another person… (SUDDEN PANIC) I am doomed! My hour is at hand!
GILBERT:	(V.O.) Then suddenly he saw something…
FOGGERTY:	(CALLING) Hallooooo!
GILBERT:	(V.O.) A dark round thing floated on the waves a mile or so from him.

	(FOGGERTY STARTS TO SWIM)
GILBERT:	(V.O.) He decided to swim towards it.
	(UNREALISTICALLY FAST SWIMMING EFFECTS)
GILBERT:	(V.O.) A retired bachelor takes a long time to swim a mile but – well, we have a tale to tell.
FOGGERTY:	(GASPING FOR BREATH) Oh, good heavens! It's alive!
GILBERT:	(V.O.) But - Mr Foggerty reflected –
FOGGERTY:	Better death from a rampaging sea monster than death from starvation.
	(SOMEBODY STARTS SWIMMING TOWARDS HIM.)
FOGGERTY:	It's – it's coming for me!
GILBERT:	(V.O.) Mr Foggerty braced himself for death. The monster resembled nothing so much as a human head in a floating plate.
DOLLY:	(BOBBING ON THE OCEAN) Hello there, funny old stick!
FOGGERTY:	(HORRIFIED) Dolly Fortescue!
DOLLY:	Ain't you pleased to see me?
FOGGERTY:	Well, it's – it's just that I'm surprised. You see, I'm not here by choice. I was wrecked on the Aurora Borealis.
DOLLY:	Me too!

FOGGERTY: You – you were on board the Aurora -?
DOLLY: Borealis? Yes, I'm a stewardess. Remember?
FOGGERTY: (CLOSE TO CRACKING UP) Oh no! This is all I need. Take me back to the Warrant Officers' Shirt-frill and Shaving-soap department – please!
DOLLY: So how are you?
FOGGERTY: I'm very cold. And this confounded rubber thing has given me a crick in the neck!
DOLLY: They're good though, aren't they? This is the third shipwreck I've survived thanks to my inflatable neckpiece. But I have to say you don't look well.
FOGGERTY: I'm freezing!
DOLLY: What you need is a tot of brandy.
FOGGERTY: Oh yes – please.
DOLLY: Here you are.

(CONTENTED GLUGGING SOUNDS FROM FOGGERTY)

FOGGERTY: Bless you, Dolly, bless you!
DOLLY: (RETRIEVING BOTTLE) Let's see. That's three shillings worth.
FOGGERTY: What?
DOLLY: Two shillings worth of brandy – and one shilling commission for the stewardess.
FOGGERTY: This is outrageous!
DOLLY: You drank it!

FOGGERTY:	Yes – but on the boat, the stewardess's commission is included.
DOLLY:	We ain't on a boat.
FOGGERTY:	Woman – where is your compassion?
DOLLY:	You're a mean old chap! And I've not forgotten you dumped me in the middle of a common in the pouring rain. I'm not going to give you anything more.
	(SILENCE APART FROM THE LAPPING WATER)
GILBERT:	(V.O.) Mr Foggerty tried to look dignified and indifferent – which is difficult when you are bobbing up and down on the sea with an india-rubber bag round your neck. Besides, Mr Foggerty was now very hungry – and he noticed that Dolly Fortescue had a large waterproof basket on her arm.
	(LAPPING WATER AND SILENCE. FINALLY:)
FOGGERTY:	(CROSSLY:) Oh, very well, here's your money.
DOLLY:	(BITING THE COIN) It's good, I'm glad to say.
FOGGERTY:	Would I cheat you?
DOLLY:	That's a good question. So can I help you to anything else? I see you looking longingly at my waterproof basket.

FOGGERTY: (RELUCTANTLY) I – I was wondering what you had in there.

DOLLY: (BRISKLY) German sausage – cucumber – carrot – bottle of barley-water – two tomatoes – a bloater – two eggs – one pound of macaroni – head of endive – stick of Spanish liquorice – and three pounds of snuff.

FOGGERTY: (AFTER A PAUSE) What are your terms for the carrot?

DOLLY: I'm afraid carrots are very dear out here. Supply and demand, you see.

FOGGERTY: So how much is the carrot?

DOLLY: One guinea.

FOGGERTY: One guinea!! (RESIGNED:) Oh very well. Here's your money.

DOLLY: And here's your carrot.

(A CARROT IS RAPIDLY CONSUMED)

DOLLY: So what are your plans now, you funny old stick?

FOGGERTY: (WARILY) That depends on your plans, Miss Fortescue?

DOLLY: Well, I am going to swim in that direction. Because I believe that's where the shore is. How about you?

FOGGERTY: (FIRMLY) Well, then, I am going to swim in the opposite direction. Because I believe that is where the shore is.

DOLLY: I think you're wrong.

FOGGERTY:	Fortified by my carrot, I will take my chance. Goodbye once more.
DOLLY:	Goodbye.

(LOTS OF VERY FAST VIGOROUS SWIMMING EFFECTS.)

GILBERT:	(V.O.) After a day and a half of vigorous swimming, Mr Foggerty reached the point of a low sandy shore.
FOGGERTY:	(RELIEVED:) Ahhhh!

(FEET WALKING OUT OF THE SEA ON TO SAND.)

GILBERT:	(V.O.) You will not be surprised to learn that Mr Foggerty was mightily relieved to feel dry land under his legs again.
FOGGERTY:	Ahhh… dry land… sand… sun… what is the one luxury I need to have with me apart from the Bible and the works of Shakespeare?
GILBERT:	(V.O.) Mr Foggerty was becoming delirious. He had, after all, lead a most sheltered life. What he really felt was extreme hunger.

(FEET ON SAND, FOLLOWED BY GULPING SOUNDS)

GILBERT:	(V.O.) Mr Foggerty picked up mussels and periwinkles and ate

	them raw. They did not agree with him. Then night fell –
	(THE OLD GAG – SOMETHING HEAVY FALLS)
GILBERT:	(V.O.) Suddenly Mr Foggerty felt very much alone. The seafood rumbled in his stomach. He wandered in a listless purposeless way across his darkened desert island –
FOGGERTY:	(SINGING GLUMLY) Here's a how-de-do! If I –
GILBERT:	(SAVAGELY) No Sullivan!
	(A SUDDEN SHRIEK AS FOGGERTY TRIPS OVER SOMETHING)
FOGGERTY:	Ouf!
GILBERT:	(V.O.) He fell over something that lay across his path.
FOGGERTY:	(STARTLED) Eeek!
GILBERT:	(V.O.) Then he became curious. He reached out his hand.
FOGGERTY:	It's a sleeping, breathing human being.
	(LOUD SNORES)
GILBERT:	(V.O.) In the dark he could see little or nothing.
FOGGERTY:	(GENTLY) Wake up… wake up…
	(THE SNORES CONTINUE)

GILBERT:	(V.O.) The creature started to stir from its slumbers. And something told Mr Foggerty that the Finger of Fate had once again picked him out.
FOGGERTY:	(IN HORROR:) Dolly Fortescue!
DOLLY:	(YAWNING) Hello, old stick! So you made it in the end!

(CUT TO A TROPICAL DAWN CHORUS.)

GILBERT:	(V.O.) When dawn broke, they surveyed their kingdom.
FOGGERTY:	No fresh water – no vegetation – principally rock.
DOLLY:	But at least it's home.
FOGGERTY:	Just us – and the inedible periwinkles.
DOLLY:	Cosy, ain't it?
FOGGERTY:	Well, as a matter of fact, it's really quite large. We should be able to live very separate existences here very easily.
DOLLY:	You in one part, me in another?
FOGGERTY:	That's the idea.
DOLLY:	Don't you like me, you funny old stick?
FOGGERTY:	What do you think?
DOLLY:	(CONFIDENTALL)) I think you've got a soft spot for me really. You're just playing hard to get.
FOGGERTY:	Miss Fortescue, I assure you I intend to keep as far away from you as possible on an island approximately twenty miles square.

DOLLY:	(BLITHELY) Very well, off you go.
FOGGERTY:	You won't follow me?
DOLLY:	Of course not.
FOGGERTY:	You see, you keep on turning up in my life.
DOLLY:	I don't plan it. It must be fate.
FOGGERTY:	Well, this time I'm taking my fate in my own hands. Goodbye, Miss Fortescue. (PAUSE) I promise I'll contact you if I catch the attention of a passing ship. It seems only fair.
DOLLY:	And I'll do the same. Goodbye, Mr Foggerty. (PAUSE) Happy hunting.
	(CROSSFADE TO WIND BLOWING, FOGGERTY SHIVERING)
GILBERT:	(V.O.) Unfortunately, Mr Foggerty was no huntsman. And periwinkles made him ill. He didn't know how to make a fire. Or build a hut. Or how to cook. Or sew handy outfits out of palm leaves. Or indeed do any of the things that resourceful castaways are supposed to do.
	(DISTANT HAMMERING. DOLLY HUMMING)
GILBERT:	(V.O.) From a distance, Mr Foggerty watch Dolly build herself a splendid hut – proof against blazing heat and tropical storm. He watched her cook

herself delicious meals with the cooking utensils she carried in her waterproof basket.

(TROPICAL RAIN STORM)

GILBERT: (V.O.) And when the rains came, he knew that once again Fate had beaten him.

(KNOCKING ON HUT DOOR)

DOLLY: (INSIDE) Come in, Mr Foggerty –

FOGGERTY: (OPENING THE DOOR, TEETH CHATTERING) Miss Fortescue, I don't want my motives to be in any way misinterpreted but –

DOLLY: But you're wet and you're hungry. Come in, I'm just grilling a couple of crocodile steaks. Half a guinea to you.

(FADE STORM. BRING UP CRACKLING BLAZE. OVER THIS:)

GILBERT: (V.O.) Thirteen years passed in this way. And then –

(OUTSIDE ACCOUSTIC, TROPICAL BIRDS ETC)

FOGGERTY: Look, look – a ship.
DOLLY: Missionaries by the look of them.

(DOLEFUL HYMN-SINGING)

GILBERT:	(V.O.) A boat full of Baptist missionaries now came on shore, bearing many bales of tracts.
	(A UNIVERSAL GROAN FROM THE MISSIONARIES)
GILBERT:	(V.O.) They were much disgusted and disappointed when they discovered the castaways were already Christians – and Protestants at that.
MISSIONARY:	Let's return to our boat, brethren. We're obviously wasting our time here.
FOGGERTY:	But you can't just leave us like this.
MISSIONARY:	But we're here to convert heathens – and you don't need conversion. You are Christian, Protestant – and no doubt, Baptist. What can we do?
FOGGERTY:	(HOPE RISING) But – I'm not Baptist – I'm Church of England.
MISSIONARY:	Ah, I sense a deal here. Will you let me make a Baptist of you, if we agree to take you with us?
FOGGERTY:	I am open to conviction.
MISSIONARY:	And what about your wife?
FOGGERTY:	She is not my wife.
	(CRIES OF HORROR FROM THE MISSIONARIES)

MISSIONARY:	Then how is it the two of you are here together alone – living as man and wife?
DOLLY:	It's a long story.
FOGGERTY:	We avoid each other as much as is humanly possible.
MISSIONARY:	This is most shocking! If we're going to rescue you from this island, you'll have to get married.
FOGGERTY:	But –
MISSIONARY:	It's a matter of principle. No wedlock – no rescue.
DOLLY:	Oh come on, Mr F., don't look so miserable. We might as well get married, mightn't we?
FOGGERTY:	(WITH A SIGH) I – I suppose so. It is the Finger of Fate.
	(CROSSFADE TO WEDDING MUSIC)
GILBERT:	(V.O.) And so – on their return to England – Frederick Foggerty and Dolly Fortescue were married. The ending of this tale, however, is not a happy one. Fate had one more cruel trick to play on Frederick Foggerty – as he would tell anyone who would listen.
	(BUSY TAVERN NOISES. FOGGERTY IN HIS CUPS)

FOGGERTY: In a week, she'd had enough of me, my wife. Can't think why. But the arrears of my pension amounted to something considerable and she ran off with the lot. I ran after her, of course, but I could never find her. (PAUSE) And I suppose now that I really want her to find her, I never shall.

(FADE FROM TAVERN INTO CLOSING MUSIC AND CREDITS)

THE END

AN ELIXIR OF LOVE

First broadcast on Radio 4 on 14th May 2003 with the following cast –

GILBERT	Jonathan Coy
REVEREND STANLEY GAY	Paul Downing
JESSIE LIGHTLY	Cathy Sara
SIR CARACTACUS	Christopher Scott
ZORAH CLARKE	Gillian Goodman
BISHOP / GROSVENOR	John Fleming

The director was SUE WILSON

(GILBERT'S VOICE HEARD MUTTERING IN AN UNDERTONE:)

GILBERT: When you're lying awake with a dismal headache, and repose is taboo'd by anxiety,
I conceive you may use any language you choose to indulge in without impropriety –

(A BRIGHT BLAST OF ONE OF THE SULLIVAN OVERTURE. GILBERT CUTS IT OFF.)

GILBERT: (V.O.) Excuse me – Gilbert without Sullivan. Thank you. (CLEARS THROAT) Today's story by W.S. Gilbert – without the collaboration of Sir Arthur Sullivan - is entitled – An Elixir of Love. The more observant among you may recognise some affinities between this tale and a comic opera I wrote called The Sorcerer. But let me emphasise. This is the original unvarnished tale – before I had to accommodate it to the musical requirements of the aforementioned Sir Arthur Sullivan. But that's quite enough of him.

(THE SOUNDS OF A RURAL IDYLL – SHEEP BLEAT, BIRDS TWITTER.)

GILBERT:	(V.O.) Ploverleigh was a picturesque little village in Dorsetshire, ten miles from anywhere. It lay in a pretty valley nestling amid clumps of elm trees – and a pleasant little trout stream ran right through it from end to end.
	(THE SOUNDS OF AN ORGAN PLAYING AND A CHOIR SINGING HEARD IN THE DISTANCE.)
GILBERT:	(V.O.) The vicar of Ploverleigh was the Honourable and Reverend Mortimer De Becheville, third son of the forty eighth Earl of Caramel. But he doesn't feature in our story because he was hardly ever there. His duties were all delegated to an estimable young curate – the Reverend Stanley Gay.
	(THE SOUND OF PEOPLE LEAVING CHURCH AND STANLEY'S VOICE GREETING THEM)
STANLEY:	Miss Pilchard, how are you? How is your dear mother? Mrs Murgatroyd, how lovely to see you fit and well etc.

	(GILBERT'S VOICE CONTINUES OVER THIS:)
GILBERT:	(V.O.) The arrangement worked admirably. The vicar paid his curate a stipend of £120 a year to do all the work while pocketing a clear profit of £1,080 for himself – while the parish had the benefit of the Reverend Stanley Gay's beautifully expressive violet eyes – as well as all his enthusiasm and idealism. For the curate was a great idealist – of which more, much more, in a few moments.
	(CROSSFADE TO EVENING IN THE COUNTRY. FAINTLY TWITTERING BIRDS, PERHAPS A PIANO PLAYING SOMETHING ROMANTIC IN THE BACKGROUND.)
JESSIE:	(DREAMILY) Oh dear, dear Stanley…
STANLEY:	My one, my only Jessie…
	(A MUTUAL SIGH)

GILBERT: (V.O.) The fortunate Reverend Gay was also engaged to be married. He loved a pretty young girl of eighteen – some four years younger than himself – with soft brown eyes and bright silky brown hair.

JESSIE: I could sit here for ever – such a lovely evening –

STANLEY: How fortunate we are…

GILBERT: (V.O.) Jessie, it must be explained, was the only daughter of Sir Caractacus Lightly, a wealthy baronet who had a large place in the neighbourhood of Ploverleigh. A genial widower, Sir Caractacus had raised no objection to the engagement – but had a certain scepticism about Mr Gay's idealistic notions. Of which we are now going to hear.

(MORE LOVERS' SIGHS, MORE DISTANT ROMANTIC PIANO MUSIC.)

JESSIE: Oh Stanley, Stanley, we are very, very happy, are we not?

STANLEY: Unspeakably happy. So happy that when I look around me, and see how many there are whose lives are embittered by disappointment – by envy, by hatred and by malice, I turn to the tranquil and unruffled calm of my own pure and happy love

	for you with gratitude unspeakable.
GILBERT:	(V.O.) By which speech, you will learn that the Reverend Stanley Gay though undoubtedly sincere was a little too fond of his own voice.
JESSIE:	(A SIGH) Oh, Stanley, I wish with all my heart that every soul on earth was as happy as we two.
STANLEY:	And why are they not, my love? And why are they not? I will tell you why they are not. Because –
JESSIE:	Yes, dear, I know why. You've explained.
STANLEY:	(PRESSING ON REGARDLESS:) It's because although Love is the great bond of union between man and woman, arbitrary obstacles too often interfere with its progress. I do not –
JESSIE:	I remember very well, dear –
STANLEY:	I do not desire to abolish Rank but I do desire that a mere difference in social rank should not be an obstacle in the way of making two young people happy.
JESSIE:	You know I agree with you. And thank heaven that my dear father has never objected to –
STANLEY:	After all, the principle is as simple as possible. I can prove it to you by figures. For example, take x to represent the abstract human being –

JESSIE:	Certainly, dear. But we took it last night.
STANLEY:	(NOW UNSTOPPABLE) Then suppose we then let x plus one, x plus two and x plus three represent three grades of high rank –
JESSIE:	I thought tonight maybe we could just sit quietly and listen to the wind sighing through the trees.
STANLEY:	But this is important. What is a duke? A mere x plus three. Could anything be more hollow?
JESSIE:	No, dear. Look - aren't the stars bright tonight? Like little jewels glistening in the sky.
STANLEY:	The Duke of Buckingham and Chandos. The title sounds very well, I grant you. But once you call him the x plus three of Buckingham and Chandos, you reduce him at once to –
JESSIE:	I know, dear. To his lowest common denominator. You know, I think I can hear an owl hooting.
STANLEY:	Jessie, I really believe you're not paying attention.
JESSIE:	Forgive me, my love, but I did think we might have one evening without talking about love breaking the class barrier.
STANLEY:	(A SNORT OF INDIGNATION) Oh very well - if you insist.
GILBERT:	(V.O.) It was their first tiff. But fortunately they very soon made

it up. Jessie, after all, was as convinced as Stanley was of the importance of love's triumph over distinctions of age and rank. She just wasn't quite so relentlessly verbose on the subject.

(CROSSFADE TO TICKING CLOCK. THEN THE OPENING OF AN INNER DOOR)

ZORAH: (ELDERLY, RUSTIC) Jessie, my dear! Come in.
JESSIE: (A LITTLE KISS) Hello, Zorah. Is Mr Gay here?
ZORAH: Sorry, dear?
JESSIE: (LOUDER) Is Mr Gay here?
ZORAH: I can't hear you.
JESSIE: I said – is Mr Gay here?
ZORAH: Roast pork and new potatoes since you ask.
GILBERT: (V.O.) Old Zorah Clarke was Stanley's cook and housekeeper. It was understood between him and Sir Caractacus Lightly that Jessie could call on the curate whenever she liked – on condition that Zorah was present during the whole time of the visit. Given that Zorah was stone deaf, this was not a particularly arduous limitation to free conversation between the lovers.

(THE DOOR OPENS AGAIN.)

STANLEY: My own!
JESSIE: My love!
STANLEY: My beloved!
JESSIE: My treasure!
ZORAH: Good idea. I'll go and make us all a nice pot of tea.

(CROSSFADE TO THE CLINK OF TEA CUPS.)

GILBERT: (V.O.) The months since the moonlit tiff had done little to abate the overwhelming enthusiasm of Stanley Gay for the cause of love conquering all considerations of wealth and age.

STANLEY: (STIRRING HIS TEA VIGOROUSLY) There really can be no doubt, Jessie. I have given lectures on the subject at mechanics' institutes and the mechanics were unanimous in their approval of my views.
JESSIE: Do have a Sally Lunn, dear. I believe Zorah's baked them specially. Didn't you, Zorah?
ZORAH: Aye, Michaelmas daisies that'll be the thing.
STANLEY: (TAKING A CAKE) Thank you, my love.

(HE CONTINUES HIS LECTURE BETWEEN MOUTHFULS OF TEA CAKE.)

STANLEY:	I have preached my doctrine in workhouses, in beer-shops, in lunatic asylums and all supported me with enthusiasm. I have addressed navvies at the roadside on the humanising advantages that would accrue to them if they married refined and wealthy ladies of rank – and not a navvy dissented.
JESSIE:	But there is a problem - isn't there, Zorah?
ZORAH:	(CHEERILY) Aye, Thomas told me they'd be starting the sheep dipping on Thursday.
STANLEY:	(HOTLY) Don't think that I don't understand the problem to which you are referring. The navvies may think it's a good idea but I don't think the Countesses will like it.
JESSIE:	My point, exactly, my love. We must look these things in the face. We cannot ignore them. We have convinced the humble mechanics and artisans – but the aristocracy holds aloof.
STANLEY:	The working man is the true Intelligence after all, Jessie. He is a noble creature when he is quite sober.
JESSIE:	But how many times have we reached this insuperable difficulty, Stanley? I despair of ever finding a solution.
STANLEY:	I have despaired too – until today. Let me set aside the remains of my delicious Sally

	Lunn and show you what I have found.
	(PLATE PUT ASIDE. THE RUSTLE OF NEWSPAPER)
JESSIE:	Why, it's a copy of The Connubial Chronicle.
STANLEY:	(SUPPRESSED EXCITEMENT) It is indeed. Now if you will be good enough to turn to page eight. -
	(THE RUSTLE OF PAGES)
STANLEY:	And then consult the boxed advertisement in its lower half.
JESSIE:	(READING) From the Earl of Market Harborough. "I am a hideous old man of eighty and everyone avoided me. I took a family bottle of your philtre, immediately on my accession to the title and estates a fortnight ago, and I can't keep the young woman off. Please send me a pipe of it to lay down." (ALARMED) Stanley, my dear, what is this?
STANLEY:	Go on.
JESSIE:	(READING) From Amelia Orange Blossom. "I am a very pretty girl of fifteen. For upwards of fourteen years past I have been without a definitely declared admirer. I took a large bottle of your philtre yesterday, and within fourteen hours a young nobleman winked at me

	in church. Send me a couple of dozen." (BRAKING OFF) Darling, what can the girl want with a couple of dozen young noblemen?
STANLEY:	I don't know – perhaps she took it too strong. But don't you see?
JESSIE:	See what, dear?
STANLEY:	The power of this love philtre?
JESSIE:	I don't think I've got to that bit yet, dear.
STANLEY:	It's an advertisement for Baylis and Grosvenor, the family magicians, astrologers and professors of the Black Art. Their shop is in St. Martin's Lane.
JESSIE:	Magicians! Black Arts! Stanley, have you taken leave of your senses?
STANLEY:	Just read on.
JESSIE:	(READING) "Our most requested item – The Patent Oxy-Hydrogen Love-at-First-Sight Draught' in bottles at one shilling and a penny ha'pence and two shillings and threepence."
STANLEY:	Don't you see? The Love Philtres that Baylis and Grosvenor advertise – they a very cheap indeed, and if we may judge by the testimonials, they are very effective.
JESSIE:	But the testimonials may lie. There may be some dreadful Faustian pact involved. There may be –

STANLEY:	There is only one thing for it, Jessie.
JESSIE:	What?
STANLEY:	We will have to go and see for ourselves. Eh, Zorah?
ZORAH:	You know what, sir? Give me a good muffin any day.

(CROSSFADE TO RATTLING COACH)

GILBERT:	(V.O.) Fortunately for the young lovers' secret plans, Sir Caractacus and his daughter were due to go to town for the season and Stanley Gay was invited to spend a fortnight with them.
STANLEY:	This is very good of you, sir.
SIR CARACTACUS:	To be honest, since my dear wife died the whole season is something of a trial and I'm not much of a support to Jessie.
JESSIE:	:Don't say that, papa.
SIR CARACTACUS:	No, no, I know I'm not the most cheerful of old fellows these days.
STANLEY:	Perhaps we should find you a new wife, sir.
SIR CARACTACUS:	No, no, I'm too old for romance.
STANLEY:	In my view, sir, nobody is ever too old for romance. Have you never hankered after another wife?

SIR CARACTACUS:	My boy, all the time. Nothing would suit me better than a loving companion of compatible tastes to soothe my declining years. But that is a world of fantasy and fairy tale, It will never happen.
STANLEY:	I wouldn't count on it, sir.
	(THE CARRIAGE RATTLES ON THEN FADES UNDER:)
GILBERT:	(V.O.) A few days later Stanley and his betrothed secretly went one afternoon to St. Martin's Lane – to visit the firm of Baylis and Grosvenor, family magicians, astrologers and professors of the Black Art. And no – they did not have anybody called John Wellington Wells working for them.
	(A SHOP DOOR CREAKS OMINOUSLY OPEN.)
STANLEY:	(NERVOUSLY) Hello!
JESSIE:	Is anybody there?
	(SILENCE.)
STANLEY:	I'll ring the bell.
	(THE SHOP BELL IS RUNG. IT ECHOES OMINOUSLY LIKE A HUGE CATHEDRAL BELL.) (HEAVY ECHOING FOOTSTEPS.)

JESSIE:	(SCARED) Someone's coming.
STANLEY:	They can't be too alarming, my love. They do advertise in all the newspapers.
	(THE FOOTSTEPS GET NEARER. THEN A VOICE – DEEP BUT OTHERWISE FRIENDLY AND MATTER OF FACT.)
GROSVENOR:	Good afternoon, sir and madam, how may I be of assistance?
GILBERT:	(V.O.) The firm of Baylis and Grosvenor stood at the very head of the London family magicians. Mr Baylis had sold himself to the Devil at a very early age and had disappeared under mysterious circumstances some years ago. But Mr Grosvenor was still very much in charge. They did what is known as a pushing trade.
GROSVENOR:	Perhaps I can interest you in a neat, well-finished divining rod or perhaps a curse. Our curses at a shilling per dozen are the cheapest in the trade. We sell dozens of them in the course of a year. Blessings are another matter – although very cheap and remarkably effective, we don't sell two in a twelve month. But the sale of penny curses, especially on Saturday night, is tremendous –

STANLEY:	(DEEP BREATH) We – we wondered if you had any fresh love philtres today.
GROSVENOR:	Plenty, sir – and highly effective too. One swig taken by the gentleman and one taken by the lady and Bob's your uncle.
STANLEY:	They fall in love?
GROSVENOR:	There and then. It's like an emotional adhesive. Plighted for ever.
JESSIE:	But what if the person who drinks it sees someone who's already fallen in love with someone else?
GROSVENOR:	Then they have to wait until another unattached party comes along and takes a swig too.
STANLEY:	Remarkable.
GROSVENOR:	No complaints yet. How many would you like?
STANLEY:	Well – let me see. There are a hundred and forty souls in my parish – say, twelve dozen.
JESSIE:	I think, dear, you are better to take a few more than you really want – in case of accidents.
GROSVENOR:	In purchasing a large quantity, sir, we would strongly advise you taking it in the wood, and drawing it off as you happen to want it. We have it in four-and-a-half and nine-gallon casks, and we deduct ten per cent for cash payments.
STANLEY:	(A MOMENTOUS DECISION) Then, Mr Grosvenor, be good enough to let me have a nine-gallon cask of Love Philtre as

	soon as possible. Send it to the Reverend Stanley Gay, Ploverleigh.
JESSIE:	(FAINTLY) My brave Stanley!
GROSVENOR:	Very good, sir.
GILBERT:	(V.O.) The curate wrote a cheque for the amount then and there. As far as he and his betrothed were concerned, the transaction was now complete. But Baylis and Grosvenor did - as I have already pointed out – a pushing trade.
GROSVENOR:	Is there any other article I can interest you in, sir.
STANLEY:	(STARTING TO LEAVE) Nothing to-day, thank you. Good afternoon.
GROSVENOR:	Have you by any chance seen our new wishing-caps? They are lined with silk and very chastely quilted, sir. We sold one to the Archbishop of Canterbury not an hour ago. Allow me to put you up a wishing cap.
STANLEY:	I tell you I want nothing more.
GROSVENOR:	Then how about one of our Flying Carpets? They're quite the talk of the town. You spread it on the ground and sit on it, and then you think of a place and you find yourself there before you can count ten.
STANLEY:	I'm afraid I've no head for heights.
GROSVENOR:	You might consider one of our Abu Hassan chests then, sir. Each chest contains a patent Hag, who comes out and

STANLEY:	prophesies disaster whenever you touch this spring. We can do you the chest complete for fifteen guineas.
(GETTING IRRITATED) Forgive me but I think you tradespeople make a great mistake in worrying people to buy things they don't want.
GROSVENOR:	(POLITELY) You'd really be surprised if you knew the quantity of things we get rid of by this means, sir.
STANLEY:	No doubt but I think you keep a great many people from coming back into your shop. Good afternoon. Come, Jessie.

(HE PULLS THE SHOP DOOR OPEN AND THEN SLAMS IT SHUT TO LOUD ECHOING EFFECT.)

GROSVENOR: What a very strange young man.

(A CART RATTLING DOWN A COUNTRY ROAD)

GILBERT: (V.O.) The nine gallon cask of Love Philtre arrived in due course – just after all our principal characters had returned to Ploverleigh. For obvious reasons, Mr Gay decided that it should be locked up in a cupboard in his library.

(SOUND OF KEY IN LOCK IN LIBRARY)

STANLEY:	There, Zorah, that's safe and sound.
ZORAH:	Never took you for a drinking man, Mr Gay.
STANLEY:	I'm not.
ZORAH:	Sorry?
STANLEY:	I'M NOT!!!
ZORAH:	That's sherry, ain't it?
STANLEY:	No, it isn't. IT ISN'T!!
ZORAH:	Thought so.
STANLEY:	It's good for people.
ZORAH:	The church clock stopped on Tuesday.
STANLEY:	It's good for people.
ZORAH:	My auntie used to paddle in the duck pond.
STANLEY:	It's not sherry. IT'S GOOD FOR PEOPLE!!
ZORAH:	Sarsaparilla then is it?
	(GROANS FROM STANLEY)
GILBERT:	(V.O.) But at least by the time Jessie arrived to discuss how to proceed, Zorah was firmly convinced of the propriety of the proceedings.
	(CROSSFADE TO STANLEY AND JESSIE IN LIBRARY.)
STANLEY:	Jessie – the question now arises – How shall we most effectually dispense the great boon we have at our command? Shall we give a party to our friends and put the Love Philtre on the table in

	decanters, and allow them to help themselves?
JESSIE:	I really don't think we can, Stanley dear.
STANLEY:	Why not?
JESSIE:	We have to be very careful not to allow any married people to taste it.
STANLEY:	True, quite true. I never thought of that. It wouldn't do at all. I am much obliged to you for the suggestion. I – I'm not sure I have thought this through as fully as I might.
JESSIE:	But surely if x plus three equals zed?
STANLEY:	Jessie, your tone is positively satirical.
JESSIE:	Because we have also to consider the engaged couples. I don't think we ought to do anything to interfere with the prospects of those who have already plighted their troth.
STANLEY:	(QUICKLY) Quite true, we have no right, no right at all. (PAUSE) But this will narrow our sphere of action very considerably.
JESSIE:	And then, of course, widows and widowers of less than one year's standing should surely be exempted from its influence.
STANLEY:	Certainly, most certainly. How true. That reflection had not occurred to me either. (A SIGH) It is clear that the dispensing of the philtre will be a very delicate operation.

JESSIE: Dearest, the more I think about it, the more I realise that it will have to be conducted with the utmost tact.

STANLEY: (NERVOUSLY) So can you think of any more exceptions?

JESSIE: Let me see. Well, there's Tibbits, papa's second groom, who drinks and really oughtn't to be allowed to marry. And there's Major Crump who uses dreadful language to ladies and Mrs Pointdextre who has such peculiar personal habits and –

STANLEY: (AGHAST) All these exceptions never occurred to me.

JESSIE: (GENTLY) On reflection, I don't think we shall ever use the whole nine gallons, dear. After all, one tablespoon is a dose.

(PAUSE. ANOTHER GLOOMY SIGH FROM STANLEY.)

STANLEY: I have just thought of another exception. Your papa.

JESSIE: But why? You know how much papa wants to marry again. You as good as promised him your help.

STANLEY: Not in a way he would understand.

JESSIE: But I understood.

STANLEY: Jessie, I too have had time for reflection. Heaven has offered me the chance of entering into the married state unencumbered with a mother-in-law. And I am

	content to accept the blessing as I find it. (PAUSE) Indeed, I prefer it so.
JESSIE:	Oh, Stanley, Stanley, never have I suspected you before of selfish motives. He longs for another wife. And yet how thankless you are. My papa is about to confer upon you the most inestimable treasure in the world – a young, beautiful and devoted wife – and yet you are prepared to withhold from him a priceless blessing that you are ready to confer upon the meanest of your parishioners.
STANLEY:	(HEROICALLY) Jessie, you have said enough. I was wrong in putting my selfish wishes before his happiness. Sir Caractacus shall marry.
JESSIE:	So – how are we to proceed?
ZORAH:	(SINGING) Three little maids from school are we, pert as a school girl well can be –
STANLEY:	Zorah – pray be quiet!
	(CROSSFADE TO THE SOUND OF LIQUID BEING POURED INTO SMALL BOTTLES.)
GILBERT:	(V.O.) It was finally decided that there was only one way in which the philtre could be safely and properly distributed. Mr Gay was to give out that he was much interested in the sale of a

very peculiar and curious old Amontillado, and small sample bottles of wine were to be circulated among such of his parishioners as were decently eligible as brides and bridegrooms. Mr Gay sent to the nearest market-town for a gross of two-ounce glass phials and Jessie and he spent a long afternoon bottling the elixir into these convenient receptacles.

(THE POURING CEASES.)

JESSIE: (WEARY SIGH) There – that's done. And now the labelling.

STANLEY: We must be careful, Jessie. Very careful. You showed me that.

JESSIE: We have been over our list of suitable recipients again and again.

STANLEY: Yes, you are right. It is what I have dreamed of. Love without distinction of age or rank. We cannot hold back now.

(SOUNDS OF WRAPPING PAPER)

GILBERT: (V.O.) The bottles were rolled up in papers and addressed to those people who had been selected as suitable for the great experiment.

(THE CLINK OF BREAKFAST THINGS).

GILBERT:	(V.O.) The next morning as Sir Caractacus Lightly sat at breakfast with Jessie, the footman informed him that Mr Gay's housekeeper wished to speak to him on very particular business. The courtly old Baronet directed that Zorah should be shown into the library and went to greet her.
	(DOOR OPENING)
SIR CARACTACUS:	(ENTERING) Ah Zorah, how can I be of assistance?
ZORAH:	If you please Sir Caractacus, and beggin' your pardon, I've come with a message from my master.
SIR CARACTACUS:	Pray be seated.
ZORAH:	Sorry, sir?
SIR CARACTACUS:	Sit down.
GILBERT:	(V.O.) The execution of the simple manoeuvre of explaining to Zorah that she was free to be seated took some ten minutes but at the end of it Sir Caractacus indicated she should reveal her purpose in coming.
ZORAH:	My master's compliments and he's gone into the wine trade, and would you accept a sample?
GILBERT	(V.O.) Mr Gay's message was somewhat subtler than this but the good Zorah's hearing had not been up to the niceties. She offered the wrapped bottle to the baronet. Sir Caractacus thought it odd but was a most obliging

sort so immediately unwrapped the bottle –

(THE NOISE OF PAPER BEING UNWRAPPED)

ZORAH: If you'll kindly taste it, sir, I'll take back any orders with which you may favour me.

SIR CARACTACUS: By all means.

(LIQUID BEING POURED INTO A GLASS)

GILBERT : (V.O.) He poured some of the liquid into a wineglass and proceeded to taste it.

SIR CARACTACUS: (SMACKING HIS LIPS) Mmm, I don't know what it is, but it's not Amontillado. Still a pleasant cordial.

(MORE LIQUID BEING POURED INTO A GLASS. OVER THIS:)

GILBERT: (V.O.) It was at this moment that Sir Caractacus, ever the genial host, decide to do something neither his daughter nor her betrothed had foreseen. He offered a glass to Zorah.

SIR CARACTACUS: Here, Zorah, see what you think.

ZORAH: Thank you, Sir Caractacus.

GILBERT: (V.O.) The old housekeeper grasped his meaning at once. She nodded, bobbed a curtsey and emptied the glass.

(ZORAH DRAINS HER GLASS.)

ZORAH: Mmmm…
SIR CARACTACUS: Mmmmmm…
ZORAH: Mmmmm…mmmmm…
SIR CARACTACUS: Mmmmmmm…mmmmmmm..

(A SUDDEN LOUD PING! CELESTIAL HARPS START TO PLAY.)

GILBERT: (V.O.) Baylis and Grosvenor had not over-stated the singular effects of the 'Patent Oxy-Hydrogen Love-at-First-Sight Draught.' Zorah's eyes met those of the good old baronet. Sir Caractacus's hard and firmly-set features gradually relaxed. Zorah blushed under the ardour of his gaze and a tear trembled on her old eyelid.

SIR CARACTACUS: (SOFTLY) You know, Zorah –
ZORAH: Pardon, Sir Caractacus –
SIR CARACTACUS: (LOUDER) You're a remarkable fine woman and singularly well preserved for your age.
ZORAH: Alas, kind, sir, I am that hard of hearin' that cannons is whispers. But I think I get your drift.
SIR CARACTACUS: (VERY LOUD) I love you, Zorah.
ZORAH: Sir Caractacus, I don't know whether it's right for a poor old woman like me to own her liking for a lordly barrownight – but a true heart us more precious

SIR CARACTACUS:	than diamonds they do say, and a lovin' wife is a crown of gold to her husband.
SIR CARACTACUS:	How true, how true…
ZORAH:	I ain't fashionable, but I'm a respectable party and can make you comfortable if nothing else.
SIR CARACTACUS:	Zorah, you are the very jewel of my hopes. My dear daughter will soon be taken from me. It lies with you to brighten my desolate old age. Will you be Lady Lightly?
ZORAH:	You'll have to speak up, dear.
GILBERT:	(V.O.) Eventually, however, Sir Caractacus by the dint of judicious mime – a skill he had learned playing charades in stately homes at Christmas time – managed to convey to Zorah his intentions. And she accepted.
ZORAH:	Yes, dearie.
SIR CARACTACUS ;	My own!
ZORAH:	My barrownight!

(A SMACKING GREAT KISS.)
(RETURN TO SOUND OF BREAKFAST THINGS.)
(THE DOOR OPENS)

GILBERT:	(V.O.) Half an hour later, Sir Caractacus returned to the breakfast room.

(SIR CARACTACUS CLEARS HIS THROAT NERVOUSLY)

SIR CARACTACUS:	Jessie, I think you really love your poor old father?
JESSIE:	Indeed, papa, I do.
SIR CARACTACUS:	Then you will, I trust, be pleased to hear that my declining years are not unlikely to be solaced by the companionship of a good, virtuous and companionable woman.
JESSIE:	My dear papa, do you really mean that – that you are likely to be married?
SIR CARACTACUS:	Indeed, Jessie, I think it is more than probable! You know you are going to leave me very soon – and my dear little nurse must be replaced or what will become of me?
JESSIE:	Oh father, I cannot tell you how happy you have made me.
SIR CARACTACUS:	And you will, I am sure, accept your new mamma with every feeling of respect and affection.
JESSIE:	Any wife of yours is a mamma of mine.
SIR CARACTACUS:	My darling! Yes, Jessie, before very long I hope to lead to the altar a bride who will love and honour me as I deserve. She is no light and giddy girl, Jessie.
JESSIE:	I'm glad, father.
SIR CARACTACUS :	No, she is a woman of sober age and staid demeanour, yet easy and comfortable ways. I am going to marry Mr. Gay's cook, Zorah.

(A LONG PAUSE)

JESSIE:	Who did you say, father?
SIR CARACTACUS:	Mr Gay's cook, Zorah. Is anything the matter?
JESSIE:	No, no, nothing at all. I'm very fond of dear Zorah.
SIR CARACTACUS:	So am I.
JESSIE:	It's just that – I thought –
SIR CARACTACUS:	What?
JESSIE:	I never thought you'd offer her a glass of the – of the sherry. I imagined you would offer it tonight at cards to Lady Fitz-Saracen.
SIR CARACTACUS:	But I don't even like Lady Fitz-Saracen.
JESSIE:	You would have done. (MAKING THE BEST OF IT) But – of course Zorah is very good and very clean and quite, quite sober in her habits. Beauty will fade but personal cleanliness is practically undying. Oh, I'm sure you will be very happy.
	(SHE BURSTS INTO TEARS)
JESSIE:	I must hurry off and tell Stanley. He will be – he will be just as delighted as I am.
	(SHE LEAVES IN TEARS SLAMMING THE DOOR BEHIND HER.)
GILBERT:	(V.O.) Meanwhile all over the village bottles that had been distributed were being opened –

	(THE RUSTLE OF PAPER)
GILBERT:	(V.O.) and the liquid poured out –
	(MULTIPLE POURINGS OF GLASSES)
GILBERT:	(V.O.) and drunk down – with extraordinary results –
VOICES:	(OVERLAPPING) Mmmm… Mmmmmm… Mmmmm…mmmmm… Mmmmmmm…mmmmmmm..
	(A SUDDEN LOUD PING! CELESTIAL HARPS START TO PLAY. FURTHER Mmmms! ARE HEARD UNDERNEATH THIS FOLLOWED BY FURTHER PINGS! THEN MORE Mmmms! AND MORE PINGS!) (THE SOUNDS OF THE CELESTIAL HARPS BECOMES POSITIVELY DEAFENING.)
GILBERT:	(V.O.) This was not perhaps the ideal moment for the Bishop of Chelsea to make an unexpected visit. Walking through the streets to pay a call at the vicarage, he could not but observe some extraordinary scenes.

(FADE UP ON BISHOP IN VICARAGE LIBRARY.)

BISHOP: My dear boy, what is happening in Ploverleigh? There seems hardly a disengaged person over thirteen years of age in the whole of Ploverleigh. Love birds everywhere. And of all ages and classes. Not necessarily paired in the way one would imagine.

STANLEY: (PROUDLY) Yes, I do believe Ploverleigh is to be the scene of a most remarkable social experiment.

BISHOP: I mean, I saw the Dowager Lady Fitz-Saracen who introduced me to her husband to be – a pleasant enough fellow, no doubt, called Alfred Creeper, who runs a public house called the 'Three Fiddlers.' And Colonel Pemberton has become engaged to little Bessie Lane, the dairy maid while his son, Willie, just back from Eton – well, I have to confess this did shock me a little - young Willie intends to marry dear old Mrs Partlet, the widow of the late sexton.

STANLEY: It worries you?

BISHOP: Well, I took me by surprise, I must confess. And I felt a little envious, to be honest with you. The single state such as I enjoy is not always a blessed one.

STANLEY: You'd like a wife of your own?

BISHOP: I try hard to be Christian but I would not be telling the truth if I did not feel a pang of envy.

STANLEY: (QUICKLY) My Lord, perhaps then you will accept a small gift from me. I would really like your opinion of this wine I have acquired some cases of.

BISHOP: (RUSTLE OF PAPER) Thank you, my boy. A little alcohol for medicinal purposes will always raise the spirits.

GILBERT: (V.O.) Soon after this, the Bishop left and Stanley could glory in his triumphs. Indeed, he had great hopes of also helping the Bishop to a nice little wife. Far be it from me to suggest that an idealist like Stanley Gay ever calculated that the Bishop had in his gift the parish of Crawleigh with the present incumbent at the point of death and the living worth £1,800 a year. But if gratitude prompted the Bishop to give him the living as a reward Stanley nobly resolved that he would not disappoint him. It was at this point that Jessie arrived.

(THE DOOR OPENS)

JESSIE: (ENTERING IN SOME AGITATION) Has Zorah returned?

STANLEY:		Yes. She seemed in excellent spirits. You wish me to summon her as our chaperone?
JESSIE:		Stanley, first I have something to tell you. Papa and Zorah are engaged.
STANLEY:		(DUMB STRUCK) Your papa and Zorah – engaged? But how?
JESSIE:		He insisted on offering her some of the philtre to try. Of course it is something of a shock to say the least. But I have been sustained by the long discussions we have had about the fact that class prejudice has no place in the world of love. Zorah is an excellent woman, however homely and –
STANLEY:		(FINALLY) But this is terrible!
JESSIE:		What is terrible?
STANLEY	:	I can't have my aged housekeeper as my mother-in-law.
JESSIE;		But Love will triumph over –
STANLEY:		Not in this case it won't. I will be a laughing stock.
JESSIE:		I cannot believe my ears. After all we have said.
STANLEY:		But consider – Zorah married to your papa! Zorah as your mother! Zorah as my mother-in-law! It's a ghastly prospect. I must telegraph Baylis and Grosvenor at once and see if there is an antidote.
JESSIE:		(STRICKEN) Oh, Stanley, and here was I trying so hard to hold to our principles. You have bitterly disappointed me.

STANLEY; JESSIE:	But Jessie – Don't attempt to follow me.
	(SHE BURSTS INTO TEARS. A DOOR SLAMS AS SHE GOES. CROSSFADE TO LIQUID BEING POURED)
GILBERT:	(V.O.) Mr Gay telegraphed to Baylis and Grosvenor and received a definitive if bleak answer. The effects of the love potion were irreversible. The Bishop meanwhile had decided to sample the cordial he had been so kindly given.
BISHOP:	(TASTING) I've tasted better but there's something about it. Waste not, want not.
	(HE DOWNS THE LIQUID. CROSSFADE TO STREET NOISES. THE BISHOP HUMS THE TUNE OF Engaged to so-and-so FROM ACT 2 OF THE SORCERER.)
GILBERT:	(V.O.) Later the Bishop went for a walk but although Ploverleigh was awash with amorous dalliance on every corner, no one was left to love the poor prelate. Understandably surrounded by courting couples he felt rather depressed and went to bed early.
	(CROSSFADE TO MORE DROPS BEING POURED)

JESSIE:	Be still, my beating heart. It must be done.
GILBERT:	(V.O.) Jessie meanwhile had returned home in a state of something akin to despair. The wonderful love she felt for Stanley seemed to be vanishing away like dew in the morning. She decided that to save her love for her betrothed, desperate remedies were needed.
JESSIE:	To renew my love – for Stanley.

(THE LIQUID IS DRUNK DOWN.)
(CROSSFADE TO COUNTRYSIDE MORNING EFFECTS – BIRDS TWITTER. FOOTSTEPS THROUGH BRACKEN)

GILBERT:	(V.O.) The next morning Jessie left home and walked across the countryside to revisit her betrothed and renew her love. The route was usually deserted but today it was not.

(THE BISHOP IS HEARD HUMMING – GETTING LOUDER AS THE FOOTSTEPS APPROACH HIM.)

GILBERT:	(V.O.) The love-lorn Bishop of Chelsea sat seated on a stile. He looked up and saw Jessie approaching.

BISHOP:	Miss Lightly –
JESSIE:	My lord…
GILBERT:	(V.O.) The consequences of this exchange were all too predictable.
JESSIE:	Mmmm…
BISHOP:	Mmmmmm…
JESSIE:	Mmmmm…mmmmm…
BISHOP:	Mmmmmmm…mmmmmmm..

(A SUDDEN LOUD PING! CELESTIAL HARPS START TO PLAY.)
(CROSSFADE TO A HEART-FELT CRY.)

STANLEY:	Aaaaaaaaaaaargh!!!!!!
GILBERT:	(V.O.) The Reverend Stanley Gay did not take the news of his beloved's betrothal to a man three times her age with as much as Christian equanimity as might have been hoped.
STANLEY:	It's not fair. She was my betrothed!
GILBERT:	(V.O.) However the Bishop was able to offer some compensation for Mr Gay's wounded feelings. The Vicar of Crawleigh died and the Bishop bestowed the living upon him. An income of £1,800 can not, of course, cure a broken heart but it certainly makes the heart ache easier to bear.

(VILLAGE ORGAN PLAYING THE WEDDING MARCH.)

GILBERT: (V.O.) The 14th of February was a great day for on that date all the couples that had been brought together through the agency of the philtre were united in matrimony by the only remaining bachelor in the place – the Reverend Stanley Gay. Very soon after Mr Gay quitted Ploverleigh for his new parish. Since the village was awash with besotted inamoratos and inamoratas, there were few who noticed him leave. Mr Gay did well at Crawleigh, of course, but he is still unmarried and, I think, likely to remain so.

(FADE FROM ORGAN TO CLOSING MUSIC AND CREDITS.)

THE END

THE BURGLAR'S TALE

First broadcast on Radio 4 on 21st May 2003 with the following cast –

GILBERT	Jonathan Coy
SEPTIMUS BELVAWNEY	John Webb
LUCRETIA BELVAWNEY	Anny Tobin
THEODORE BELVAWNEY	Michael Onslow
STONELEIGH	Kim Durham
BELINDA STONELEIGH	Alexandra Lilley
JOHN DAVIS	Stephen Boswell

The director was SUE WILSON

	(GILBERT'S VOICE HEARD MUTTERING IN AN UNDERTONE:)
GILBERT:	For your brain is on fire – the bedclothes conspire of usual slumber to plunder you: First your counterpane goes, and uncovers your toes, and your sheet slips demurely from under you –
	(A BRIGHT BLAST FROM ONE OF THE SULLIVAN OVERTURES. GILBERT CUTS IT OFF.)
GILBERT:	(V.O.) Excuse me – this is Gilbert without Sullivan. Thank you. (CLEARS THROAT) Today's tale by W.S.Gilbert - unencumbered by the musical embellishments of Sir Arthur Sullivan – is entitled The Burglar's Story. It is a highly moral tale from which I trust you will all derive a great deal of edification.
	(GENTEEL PIANO MUSIC IN THE BACKGROUND. OVER THIS A GRUFF MIDDLE-AGED MALE VOICE:)
BELVAWNEY:	(AS IF WRITING) Dear Sir, I am a widow of thirty-five living in reduced circumstances with

	my adorable blond curly-headed children, Nell and Willy. My husband was a military man garnished with honours beyond measure but now alas dead leaving us all but destitute. Indeed I fear that my little darlings may not be long for this world until someone comes to our aid…
GILBERT:	(V.O.) In the charmingly winding alleys and streets of the Seven Dials district of London lived a hard-working couple by the name of Septimus and Lucretia Belvawney.
	(PIANO MUSIC CONTINUES)
BELVAWNEY:	(AS IF WRITING) Dear Madam, I am reluctant to seek your aid in a delicate matter but I see no other way in which to extricate myself from my dreadful predicament. It pains me to ask anyone for money but I am at my wits' end. A young girl of but eighteen I have devoted my life to caring for my dear white-headed mother who is now at death's door if I cannot raise the sums needed for her cure…
GILBERT:	(V.O.) Mr Septimus Belvawney was a highly distinguished begging-letter writer, much respected amongst the masters of that thriving trade for his trenchant prose and vivid

	imagination. Mr Belvawney, it was alleged, could get blood out of a stone.
BELVAWNEY:	(AS IF WRITING) Honoured Sir, my hand is barely strong enough to lift up my pen so parlous is my condition. A young man of blameless life and great artistic promise, I have been struck low by undeserved catastrophe. Much as I hate to approach anyone with an appeal for money…

(THE PIANO MUSIC STOPS. MRS BELVAWNEY SPEAKS:)

MRS BELVAWNEY:	How go your labours, Septimus, dear?
BELVAWNEY:	I will soon be done, my love. I just have to recopy the starving orphan's last desperate appeal. I fear I haven't made the writing quite shaky enough.
MRS BELVAWNEY:	Ah, Septimus, you are such a perfectionist. People simply do not appreciate the craftsmanship behind your work.
BELVAWNEY:	Nor yours, my love.

(CROSSFADE TO A BUSY STREET, PEOPLE PASSING)

MRS BELVAWNEY:	(MAKING HER WAY THROUGH THE CROWD) Excuse me, sir. Excuse me. I have to get home to my little girl

	who is sick… Excuse me… Oh, I feel faint….
	(A FLUTTERY SHRIEK FOLLOWED BY A BODY HITTING THE PAVEMENT. IMMEDIATELY A BABBLE OF CONCERNED VOICES:)
PASSER-BY:	Are you all right, madam? Madam - can you hear me?
MRS BELVAWNEY:	(FEEBLY) Ahhhh…
PASSER-BY:	Shall I call for a doctor? Madam – madam –
	(THE BABBLE OF VOICES CONTINUES UNDER:)
GILBERT:	(V.O.) Mrs Belvawney's speciality was fainting in public places. Always impeccably dressed in an appropriately sober and respectable style, her phantom seizures were a spectacle worth study by all students of the art of deception.
MRS BELVAWNEY:	(WEAKLY) Where am I? What has happened?
PASSER-BY:	I am sorry to see you in this state, ma'am. Can I be of any assistance?
MRS BELVAWNEY:	No, no, if you could just help me to my feet.
PASSER-BY:	Of course, ma'am, of course.
	(MUCH GRUNTING AS MRS BELVAWNEY IS HELPED TO HER FEET.)

PASSER-BY:	There, ma'am. How do you feel?
MRS BELVAWNEY:	Much better, thank you, kind sir. I had better get home to my ailing daughter and –

(ANOTHER FLUTTERY SHRIEK FOLLOWED BY ANOTHER THUD AS MRS B HITS THE PAVEMENT.)

GILBERT:	(V.O.) Mrs Lucretia Belvawney's second faints were if anything even more impressive demonstrations of her art than her first faints. They never failed to produce a great display of concern in those who observed them.

(MORE BABBLE OF VOICES. AGAIN THE PASSER-BY:)

PASSER-BY:	Madam – speak to me.
MRS BELVAWNEY:	Where am I? Where is my adored Angelina?
PASSER-BY:	Madam, you cannot possibly return home on foot in this condition. You must take a cab.
MRS BELVAWNEY:	Oh sir, alas, I cannot possibly afford such a luxury. Even a loaf of bread stretches our means to the utmost.
PASSER-BY:	Then I shall give you the money.
MRS BELVAWNEY:	Oh, no, sir, I couldn't possibly. You have been kind enough already.
PASSER-BY:	I insist.

MRS BELVAWNEY:	I cannot possibly take money from you.
GILBERT:	(V.O.) But of course in the end she always did.

(CROSSFADE TO CAB DOWN STREET)

GILBERT:	(V.O.) The price of a cab may not seem much for such an elaborate performance but as Mrs Belvawney always seemed to live on the other side of London from where she had fainted, the proceedings were actually quite profitable. She paid off the cab once she was out of sight of her benefactor and as often as not was fainting again within a few hundred yards.

(CROSSFADE BACK TO THE PIANO PLAYING.)

GILBERT:	(V.O.) Mr and Mrs Belvawney lived a hard-working and prosperous existence for a number of years. So prosperous did that it became possible for Mrs Belvawney to retire from the fainting business and for them to exist solely on the ingenuity of her dear Septimus.
BELVAWNEY:	(AS IF WRITING) Reverend sir, as a young woman of a fervently religious disposition, I beseech you – (STOPS) no, no –

	implore you to listen to my sad tale…
GILBERT:	(V.O.) But there was another reason behind Lucretia Belvawney's retirement.

(CROSSFADE PIANO TO SOUNDS OF BABY CRYING.)

GILBERT:	(V.O.) In the eighth year of their marriage, she gave birth to a bouncing baby boy – their pride and joy.
BELVAWNEY:	Ahhhhh… cootchy-coo
MRS BELVAWNEY:	Cootchy – cootchy – coo
BELVAWNEY:	Bless him…ah, bless him
MRS BELVAWNEY:	Bless him, bless him, bless him.
BOTH:	Ahhhhhhhh.

(SOUNDS OF HAPPY GURGLING BABY)

GILBERT:	(V.O.) The baby boy was named Theodore in honour of his paternal grandfather who had, in his day, been a highly distinguished blackmailer and poison-pen letter before his untimely demise in one of Great Britain's best-known prisons. From the first the Belvawneys intended that their son should have the very best of everything.

(CROSSFADE TO MRS BELVAWNEY SINGING A LULLABY TO A QUIETLY SNORING BABY.)

MRS BELVAWNEY:	Bye, baby bunting… father's gone a hunting…
BELVAWNEY:	Oh, Lucretia, what a fine bonny boy he is. Where once I wrote ten begging letters a day now I will write thirty in order than he shall never want.
MRS BELVAWNEY:	My dear, what a good father you are.
BELVAWNEY:	And what a good mother you are.
BOTH:	Mmmmmmm…
	(STICKY KISSES)
GILBERT:	(V.O.) Time passed and as Theodore attended his infant school, he already showed signs of great promise.
	(CROSSFADE TO CHILDREN PLAYING IN BACKGROUND)
MRS BELVAWNEY:	(EXCITEDLY) Oh Septimus, Septimus, do see what dear little Theodore has brought back from school. He has been copying the alphabet into his note book.
BELVAWNEY:	(IN WONDER) A … B… C… Ah, he writes a beautiful clear hand, Lucretia.
MRS BELVAWNEY:	No doubt where he gets his talent for copying from, dear.
BELVAWNEY:	Maybe we should get him practising forging signatures

MRS BELVAWNEY:	since he seems to have a talent for it. No, no, my dear, let us wait. Let us not push him too far in one direction when he may yet display rare talents in many others.
	(CROSSFADE TO OLDER CHILDREN PLAYING A GAME.)
GILBERT:	(V.O.) And indeed his mother's words proved wise. Young Theodore did brilliantly at his examinations thanks to his exceptional ability at cheating. Nobody knew half as well as he how to smuggle the relevant text book into the examination room. At sports too, he thrived –
	(SOUNDS OF CHEERING)
GILBERT:	(V.O.) He won many trophies by his remarkable skill at nobbling his most dangerous rivals beforehand with mouse poison and bits of string. As his infant school days came to a close his parents had no doubt in their minds as to where he should go next.
	(CROSSFADE BACK TO THE PIANO PLAYING)

MRS BELVAWNEY:	(AT THE PIANO) Theodore has a glorious future ahead of him, Septimus.
BELVAWNEY:	Yes – and we must give him of the very best.
MRS BELVAWNEY:	(EXCITED) You mean you have decided?
BELVAWNEY:	Yes, there's only one educational establishment worthy of our boy. I have put his name down for Eton.
	(THE ETON BOATING SONG VERY LOUD.)
GILBERT:	(V.O.) The Eton Boating Song I would like to remind you all was <u>not</u> written by Sir Arthur Sullivan,
	(AS THE BOATING SONG FADES, BRING IN THE SOUND OF CRICKET ON A GREEN.)
GILBERT:	(V.O.) Theodore Belvawney continued to fulfil his early promise. The methods he had employed in his infant school to pass exams and win races served him well in the more august portals of Eton College. And here he had an opportunity to profit mightily from his ability to cheat at cards and blackmail boys who had committed indiscretions of which he had got wind. Let us pass a veil over the sort of

	indiscretions public school boys sometimes get up to for it has never been our way to dwell upon the unsavoury.
	(CROSSFADE TO THE ETON CHOIR SINGING A HYMN)
GILBERT:	(V.O.) And so Theodore Belvawney gained golden opinions – and golden pay-offs – and left Eton College trailing clouds of glory.
	(CROSSFADE BACK TO DOMESTIC PIANO)
MRS BELVAWNEY:	Oh my boy, my clever, clever boy.
BELVAWNEY:	Theo, I'm proud of you.
THEODORE:	(POSHER THAN HIS PARENTS) Thanks awfully for the homecoming, mater and pater. You can't expect a fellow to get all dewy-eyed but I can tell you I'm jolly glad to be back in the old family home.
BELVAWNEY:	Beautifully put, Theo.
MRS BELVAWNEY:	My dear manly boy!
THEODORE:	So what now, eh, mater and pater? What's next up?
BELVAWNEY:	Your mother and I have just been discussing this very thing.
MRS BELVAWNEY:	There seems little doubt in our minds.
THEODORE:	Are you proposing what I hope you're proposing?

BELVAWNEY:	I think we are. (PAUSE) We are going to send you to Cambridge University.
THEODORE:	Oh, bravo, pater!
MRS BELVAWNEY:	My clever boy!
	(MUCH MUTUAL CONGRATULATION. THEN OVER THIS:)
GILBERT:	(V.O.) But at this moment the family hopes were struck a cruel blow.
	(A HEAVY KNOCKING ON THE FRONT DOOR.)
MRS BELVAWNEY:	See who it is, Septimus.
	(THE FRONT DOOR IS OPENED.)
POLICEMAN:	Are you Septimus Aloysius Belvawney?
BELVAWNEY:	I – I may be –
POLICEMAN:	Otherwise known as Mrs Edith Carberry, the Reverend Elias Bampton Boo, Miss Alice Brown, Little Jamie Merryweather, Captain Parklebury Todd, Ellen McJones Aberdeen….
GILBERT:	(V.O.) After many years of honest and discreet toil, luck had finally run out for Septimus Aloysius Belvawney –
POLICEMAN:	Also known as Mrs Josephine Golightly, the Dowager Countess of Sangazure, Master

	Thomas Winterbottom Hance, Barnaby Payle, B.A, Lieutenant Colonel Flare (retired), Dame Carruthers, Reginald Bunthorne, Archibald Grosvenor –
	<u>(THE POLICEMAN'S VOICE FADES AWAY UNDER THE CLANGING OF A LOCK IN A JAIL.)</u>
GILBERT:	(V.O.) Mr Belvawney was sentenced to two years' hard labour. The hard-hearted Judge was unmoved by his counsel's plea for mercy on account of Mr Belvawney's blameless family life and unfailing industry. Perversely he chose to depict Mr Belvawney as a leech upon the good will of society, His cruel words bit far harder than any sentence. But Mr Belvawney had no choice but to take his punishment.
	<u>(FOOTSTEPS ALONG A STONE CORRIDOR THEN AN IRON DOOR IS UNLOCKED AND OPENED.)</u>
JAILER:	Someone to see you, Belvawney.
THEODORE:	Pater!
BELVAWNEY:	Theo! My dear Theo!
JAILER:	I'll wait outside.
BELVAWNEY:	Thank you, thank you.

JAILER:	Personally, I can't abide these touching family scenes. They make me feel sick. You've got five minutes.
THEODORE:	Here is a guinea.
JAILER:	You've got ten minutes.

(THE IRON DOOR IS SLAMMED SHUT AND LOCKED.)

THEODORE:	Well, pater, this is a bit of a poser, ain't it? I'd brought some stout files with me to help you get out but the heartless warders searched me all too thoroughly and embarrassingly discovered the secret hiding place.
BELVAWNEY:	Where was that, my boy?
THEODORE:	I don't think you really want to know, pater. So sorry you're just going to have to serve your sentence.
BELVAWNEY:	I'm afraid this means we're not going to be able to send you to Cambridge, Theo.
THEODORE:	No point crying over spilt milk, eh, pater?
BELVAWNEY:	That's the spirit, my boy.
THEODORE:	I'll just have to live off mamma until you can get out and start earning for us all again. I'm trying to persuade mamma to go back into the fainting business. After all, it's a shame to waste a talent like that but she says she don't have the figure for it any more but –

BELVAWNEY:	Theodore, I am afraid I have some bad news for you.
THEODORE:	Bad news! What about?
BELVAWNEY:	I doubt whether the money I have concealed will last even six months, let alone the two years the heartless Judge has condemned me to.
THEODORE:	Then what are we going to do?
BELVAWNEY:	Theodore, my dear boy, I don't know how to break this to you. But you are going to have to get a job.
THEODORE:	(IN HORROR) A job! Pater – did you say a job?
BELVAWNEY:	I did.
THEODORE:	But I have had a highly expensive education equipping me to sit around all day doing nothing and being perfectly foul to all the servants – and now you say I have to work – to earn my living?
BELVAWNEY:	I'm sorry but there is no choice. Now of course I'm not suggesting that you take on some menial occupation without prospects. With your education and ability, it is essential that you have a calling – a proper career.
THEODORE:	Well, I suppose if you put it more as having a career then I suppose it's rather more appropriate and gentlemanly for an old Etonian.
BELVAWNEY:	Now I had thought of training you up to follow me in the

	begging-letter writing business but –
THEODORE:	Not a lot of prospects in that at present, are there, pater?
BELVAWNEY:	All the same, I could take you in hand and teach you the profession
THEODORE:	Can't say I'm keen, pater.
BELVAWNEY:	I understand your reluctance. It's an over crowded market and the competition's hotting up. <u>(PAUSE)</u> Besides, I doubt whether it is a satisfactory calling for an athletic young fellow like you. I'm sorry, Theodore, I was being selfish.
THEODORE:	So we're agreed then, pater, I'm not cut out for your profession. So what am I going to do?
BELVAWNEY:	That, dear boy, is up to you. I should like you to consult your own tastes on so important a matter as the choice of a profession.
THEODORE:	Thanks, pater. I'll give it a thought. After all, I don't want to rush into anything.
BELVAWNEY:	<u>(IMPATIENCE FINALLY BREAKING THROUGH)</u> All I will say is this – if you can get this into your head. If you don't choose yourself a solid profession soon then you'll be dead of starvation before I'm out of prison.
THEODORE:	Oh come on, pater, no need to –
BELVAWNEY:	<u>(FIERCELY)</u> Get on with it, you idle parasite,

THEODORE:	(SHOCKED) Pater!
	(THE IRON DOOR IS UNLOCKED AGAIN.)
JAILER:	Time's up!
	(CROSSFADE TO TAVERN NOISES)
GILBERT:	(V.O.) Young Theodore Belvawney took himself off to a hostelry to consider his position. Up to now he had been without care. Now he faced the most momentous decision of his young life. He sipped his beer and considered his options.
	(THEODORE SIPS HIS BEER.)
THEODORE:	Well, there's the Army I suppose –
GILBERT:	(V.O.) He began there as he had to begin somewhere –
THEODORE:	The uniform would be nice but I really don't want to go round killing people. There's the Navy, of course –
GILBERT:	(V.O.) He took another sip.
THEODORE:	(SIPPING) But I've never liked the idea of going to sea. I have a feeling it wouldn't agree with me. There's the Church, of course, but that's not really a respectable occupation for somebody of my education and

GILBERT:	background. And then there's the Bar, of course – (V.O.) For a moment he hesitated –
THEODORE:	(ANOTHER SIP) No. Not after what they did to the dear old pater. They're all nothing but a bunch of crooks.

(CROSSFADE TO THE TAVERN SOUNDS LATER.)

GILBERT:	(V.O.) The evening progressed and Theodore Belvawney began to realise how very difficult it was to find a profession that was both honourable and rewarding.
THEODORE:	(STILL DRINKING) I suppose there's always forgery. The forgers I've met through the parents have always been men of great breeding and education. The trouble is I may have had a forgers' hand while I was at infant school. But Eton's put pay to that. I've a regular Eton hand. It's as much as I can do to forge my own name.

(CROSSFADE TO LATER AND THEODORE DRUNKER)

THEODORE:	(STILL DRINKING) There's Cornish Wrecking, of course. I've heard good things about that. After all, you don't need to go to sea. You just extinguish all the lighthouses and beacons and

	let the ships wreck themselves. Yes, there's something to be said for Cornish wrecking. I've heard very good reports of the very gentlemanly pirates who reside in Penzance. (A SUDDEN BURST OF SULLIVAN'S MUSIC FOR THE PIRATES OF PENZANCE.)
GILBERT:	(V.O.) (FURIOUS) Excuse me – this is Gilbert without Sullivan – remember? We will have no Sullivan here. (THE MUSIC CUTS OFF ABRUPTLY)
GILBERT:	(V.O.) Thank you. (CLEARS THROAT) Anyway, Theodore decided against Cornish wrecking since he had heard the weather in Cornwall was often rather inclement. It was only at the end of the evening that he came to the conclusion that you may consider rather obvious in view of the title of our story.
THEODORE:	(DRUNK) I think I should like to be - a burglar! (CROSSCUT TO PRISON ACCOUSTIC.)
BELVAWNEY:	Yes, yes, I think that's an excellent idea, Theodore. Burglary is a fine manly

THEODORE:	profession. But it is dangerous, sometimes highly dangerous. Just dangerous enough to be exciting, no more, in my view, pa. Not half as dangerous as the Eton Wall Game.
BELVAWNEY:	Well, if you've set your heart on it, we'll see what can be done. I'll send a letter to Frederick Stoneleigh. No doubt you've heard me talk of him.
THEODORE:	Of course.
BELVAWNEY:	Then you know that he is a burglar of the very highest professional standing. He is also an old friend. I will write and ask if he will take you on.

(CROSSFADE TO TICKING CLOCK)

GILBERT:	(V.O.) Mr Belvawney was always prompt with pen and ink and wrote to Mr Stoneleigh that very night. Within a week Theodore was formally articled to him with a view – if things worked out – to ultimate partnership.

(THE TICKING CLOCK CONTINUES UNDER:)

STONELEIGH:	(MIDDLE-AGED, GENTEEL) I am going to work you hard, Theodore. Burglary is a jealous mistress. She will tolerate no rivals.
THEODORE:	I appreciate that, sir.

STONELEIGH:	She exacts the undivided devotion of her worshippers.
THEODORE:	(SLIGHT SIGH) Indeed, sir.
GILBERT:	(V.O.) Let it not be imagined from Theodore's sigh that he was no longer enthusiastic about his new profession. Far from it. But Mr Stoneleigh had a daughter called Belinda – a very attractive daughter – and Theodore could not help feeling that it was a pity he was not going to have any time free to worship Belinda as well.
	(THE CLINK OF JEWELLERY BEING SORTED)
GILBERT:	(V.O.) In the fair and delicate hands of Belinda was placed an important task. It was she who sorted and assessed all the jewels and plate that the firm of Stoneleigh accumulated in the course of its labours. And it was also she who fenced it for the firm with a professionalism which was much admired – particularly by Theodore Belvawney.
	(CLINKING CONTINUES. THEODORE APPROACHES.)
THEODORE:	Can I by any chance be of any assistance, Miss Belinda.
BELINDA:	No, thank you, Mr Belvawney, but thank you for offering.

THEODORE:	You're sure there's nothing I can do?
BELINDA:	Nothing at all.
GILBERT:	(V.O.) But there was a look in Miss Stoneleigh's eye that gave Theodore some hope he was not despised. But Mr Stoneleigh had not lied about the rigorous demands of the burglar's profession. Every morning at ten o'clock Theodore presented himself at Stoneleigh's chambers in New Square, Lincoln's Inn and until twelve he had at least the opportunity of assisting the lovely Belinda with the correspondence.
BELINDA:	(DICTATING) Dear Sir –
THEODORE:	(SOFTLY) Or dear, dear Madam –
BELINDA:	No, no, Theodore, that would not be appropriate.
	(THE DOOR OPENS)
STONELEIGH:	(CALLING) Mr Belvawney – please.
	(CROSSFADE TO TWO PAIRS OF FEET WALKING DOWN STREET)
GILBERT:	(V.O.) At twelve Theodore went prospecting with Mr Stoneleigh.
THEODORE:	That one!
STONELEIGH:	No, no – look at that guard dog!
THEODORE:	Then the one next door!
STONELEIGH:	Have you seen that broken glass?

(NOW IT'S ONLY ONE PAIR OF FEET.)

GILBERT: (V.O.) From two to four he had to devote himself to private study. He had to find out all particulars necessary for a scientific burglary in any given house. At first he did this for practice and with no view to an actual attempt.

(BACK WITH THE CLOCK)

STONELEIGH: Right – No. 3 Primrose Mews – now I want all the particulars you've observed about the house and its inmates – their comings and goings, the number of servants, any servants who are male and, if so, whether they slept in the basement or not. So – off you go and let's see how you've done.

THEODORE: (VERY FAST) Mother, father, daughter, three servants – one male – sleeps in the attic but carries a blunderbuss, parents generally go to bed around eleven, the daughter around nine…

GILBERT (V.O.) Mr Stoneleigh would compare Theodore's information with his own facts and compliment or blame him as he might deserve. He was a strict master but always just, kind and courteous, as became a highly polished gentleman of the old school.

(THE CLINK OF TOOLS GOING INTO A BAG)

STONELEIGH: Jemmy... pistols... crowbar... cosh... patent safe opener... yes that's it.

BELINDA: Good luck, father. (PAUSE) Good luck, Theodore.

THEODORE: Thank you, Belinda. Can I just say –

STONELEIGH: No time now, Theodore, we must be going.

(A PANE OF GLASS BEING DISCREETLY SMASHED AND PULLED ASIDE)

GILBERT: (V.O.) After a year's probation, Theodore accompanied Mr Stoneleigh on several expeditions and had the happiness to believe he was of some little use. But then one night disaster struck –

THEODORE: Take that, you villain!

(A PISTOL GOES OFF. A SCREAM AND A THUD.)

GILBERT: (V.O.) On this particular night Theodore forgot his dark lantern. During the course of the burglary he took aim at what he believed was the master of the house come to apprehend him. Unfortunately in the dark he made a mistake. The man he had shot was in fact his own master who expired a few minutes later on top of a grand piano.

(HEAVY GASPING FOR BREATH)

STONELEIGH: Theodore, my boy, it looks like I'm a goner.
THEODORE: I'm very sorry, sir. It was a genuine mistake.
STONELEIGH: Accidents happen. No hard feelings. All I ask is – look after Belinda. The money is hers apart from a three thousand pound bequest to the Society for Providing More Bishops.
THEODORE: And the business –
STONELEIGH: Aaaargh!!
THEODORE: I'm sorry, I didn't quite catch that?
STONELEIGH: Aaaaaaaaaargh!!!
THEODORE: You mean it's mine?
STONELEIGH: (DEATH RATTLE) Ohhhhhhhhhh…
THEODORE: I think I shall take it as a yes,

(FUNERAL MUSIC)

BELINDA: (WEEPING) Oh, father, dear father-
GILBERT: (V.O.) Mr Stoneleigh was much mourned by the criminal community of which he had been such a distinguished pillar. Mr Belvawney sent a letter of condolence – one of those rare letters he is known to have

MRS BELVAWNEY:	signed with his own name. Mrs Belvawney came and fainted appropriately. Ohhhh!
	(A DISCREET THUD. FUNERAL MUSIC FADES UNDER:)
GILBERT:	(V.O.) All in all, he was given the best send-off that stolen money could buy. Then began the serious task of going through the ledgers, daybooks, memoranda and papers of the business.
	(THE RUSTLE OF PAPERS BEING SORTED)
BELINDA:	Oh poor dear father, how painstakingly he has kept all this – nothing is missing, all is in such good order – and yet –
THEODORE:	What is it that troubles you, Belinda?
BELINDA:	After all his efforts over the years, there doesn't seem to be that much money in the business. Barely enough for me to live on for three months. Certainly not enough for us to get married on. If we are going to get married, that is.
THEODORE:	I told you it was your father's dying wish.
BELINDA:	Very well, if you say so, but
THEODORE:	But what, my love?

BELINDA:	I know I am but a simple maiden with no knowledge of the world outside of fencing stolen goods but it does seem to me that there is only one way ahead.
THEODORE:	And what is that, my love?
BELINDA:	You must go and start burgling as quickly as you possibly can.

(CROSSFADE TO TURNING PAGES OF LARGE BOOK)

THEODORE:	Ah, here we are – this sounds ideal. (READING) "No.102 Thurloe Square. Occupant – John Davis, bachelor. Occupation – Designer of Dados. Age – 86. Physical peculiarities – very feeble, eccentric, drinks, snores, Evangelical."
BELINDA:	Dear father – always so very precise.
THEODORE:	"Servants – two housemaids, one cook, all female. Particulars of servants – Pretty housemaid called Rachel – goes out for beer at 9 p.m. Open to attentions."
BELINDA:	Not from you, I trust. Except in the line of duty.
THEODORE:	(READING ON) "Ugly housemaid called Bella. Presbyterian. Open to attentions. Snores. Elderly cook. Primitive Methodist. Open to attentions. Snores."
BELINDA:	And the fastenings?

THEODORE:	I'm coming to that. (READING ON) "Chubb's locks on street door, chain and bolts. Bars to all basement windows. Practicable approach from third room, ground floor, which is shuttered and barred, but bar has no catch, and can be raised with table knife."
BELINDA:	Ideal for you who are not as experienced as dear papa.
THEODORE:	Indeed. (READING) "Valuable Contents of House – Presentation plate from grateful aesthetes. Gold repeater. Two diamond rings. Complete edition of Bradshaw's Railway Guide from 1834 to the present time, 588 volumes, bound in limp calf."
BELINDA:	You must go there tonight.
	(CUT TO THE CLANK OF TOOLS BEING CHECKED.)
THEODORE:	Two crowbars, a bunch of skeleton keys, a centre-bit, a dark lantern, a box of silent matches, some putty, a life preserver – and a table knife.
GILBERT:	(V.O.) That night – for it was mid-winter – it was bitterly cold and the snow was already thick on the ground.
THEODORE:	My love, do you think in view of the inclement conditions it would be wise if I postponed this exploit for another night?

GILBERT: (V.O.) But the gentle Belinda was not to be deterred.

BELINDA: It is only matter of wrapping up warmly, Theo my love. Do you have everything now?

THEODORE: Yes – I think so.

BELINDA: Then be off at once, my brave betrothed. Succeed in your task and return to me laden with rich booty.

THEODORE: My own!

(A KISS)

THEODORE: Of course, my love, you do realise that there is a possibility that I may not succeed. There is a certain amount of risk involved. Will you wait for me whatever happens?

BELINDA: I promise to wait for a reasonable amount of time. You can't expect more than that, can you?

(ANOTHER KISS)

BELINDA: (FIRMLY) Now off you go.
THEODORE: Farewell, my love.

(THE DOOR IS OPENED. IMMEDIATELY A HUGE SNOW STORM EXPLODES.)

GILBERT: (V.O.) The night was bitterly cold with at least a foot of snow on the ground and more to come. Nevertheless aided by Mr Stoneleigh's impeccable

	particulars, Theodore got to the house in question –
	(WINDOW BEING LEVERED OPEN WITH KNIFE AND PUSHED UP. SNOW STORM FADING)
GILBERT:	(V.O.) Theodore got in through the third room on the ground floor without any difficulty and then made his way into the dining room –
	(DOOR PUSHED QUIETLY OPEN. SOFT FOOTSTEPS.)
GILBERT:	(V.O.) There was the presentation plate, sure enough – about 800 ounces of it. Theodore took hold of this and started to tie it up so that he could carry it without attracting attention.
	(THE CLANK OF PLATE BEING WRAPPED.)
GILBERT:	(V.O.) He was just finishing when he heard a slight cough behind him.
DAVIS:	Ahem!
GILBERT:	(V.O.) He turned and saw a dear old silver-haired gentleman in a dressing-gown standing in the doorway. The venerable gentleman covered him with a revolver. Theodore's first

DAVIS:	impulse was to rush and brain him with his life-preserver. (SWEETLY) Please don't move – or you're a dead man. (PAUSE) I take it that you're a burglar.
THEODORE:	I have that honour, yes. Now –
GILBERT:	(V.O.) And he made for his pistol pocket.
DAVIS:	(SWEETLY) Please don't move. Thank you ever so much. Now I have often wished to have the pleasure of encountering a burglar, in order to test a favourite theory of mine as to how persons of that class should be dealt with. But you mustn't move.
THEODORE:	I – I shall be happy to be of assistance. Provided of course that you will allow me to leave the house unmolested when your experiment is at an end.
DAVIS:	If you obey me promptly, you shall be at perfect liberty to leave the house.
THEODORE:	You will neither give me into custody, nor take steps to pursue me?
DAVIS:	On my honour as a Designer of Dados.
THEODORE:	Very well then let us proceed.
DAVIS:	Now stand up and stretch out your arms at right angles to your body.
THEODORE:	Suppose I don't?
DAVIS:	Then I'm afraid I send a bullet through your left ear.
THEODORE:	But permit me to observe –

(A REVOLVER SHOT.)

THEODORE:	Ow!
GILBERT:	(V.O.) A ball cut off the lobe of his left ear. The ear smarted but under the circumstances Theodore thought it better to comply with the whimsical old gentleman's wishes.
DAVIS:	Very good. Now do as I tell you, promptly and without a moment's hesitation, or I fear I shall shoot off the lobe of your right ear. Throw me that life-preserver.
THEODORE:	But –
DAVIS:	(THE CLICK OF THE REVOLVER) Promptly please.
GILBERT:	(V.O.) Theodore tossed his life-preserver to the old man. He caught it neatly.
DAVIS:	Now take off your coat and throw it to me.
GILBERT:	(V.O.) Theodore took off his coat and threw it diagonally across the room.
DAVIS:	Now the waistcoat. (PAUSE) Now the boots –
THEODORE:	They're shoes. I would never wear boots indoors.
DAVIS:	Shoes then. (PAUSE) Trousers-
THEODORE:	Come, come, I say –

(A REVOLVER SHOT.)

THEODORE:	Ow!
GILBERT:	(V.O.) The lobe of his other ear came off. With all his

	eccentricity the old gentleman was a man of his word. Unfortunately for Theodore, his revolver happened to be in the right-hand pocket of his trousers.
DAVIS:	And now the rest of your drapery.
THEODORE:	Oh very well….
GILBERT:	(V.O.) Reluctantly Theodore yielded the remainder of his clothing to the elderly gentleman.
THEODORE:	What happens now?
DAVIS:	Just give me a moment –
GILBERT:	(V.O.) The old gentleman tied up Theodore's clothes in the table cloth. Then made for the door with the bundle under his arm.
DAVIS:	There – I won't detain you any longer.
THEODORE:	But what is to become of me without my clothing?
DAVIS:	Really, I've no idea.
THEODORE:	You promised me my liberty.
DAVIS:	Certainly. Pray don't let me trespass any further on your time.
THEODORE:	But it's freezing –
DAVIS:	(IGNORING HIM) You will find the street door open – or if from force of habit you prefer the window, you will have no difficulty in clearing the area railings.
THEODORE:	But I can't go out like this! Won't you give me something to put on?

DAVIS:	No, nothing at all. Good night.
	(THE DOOR SLAMS SHUT.)
GILBERT:	(V.O.) The quaint old man left the room with the bundle. Theodore went after him but he found he had locked an inner door that lead upstairs.
	(FUTILE RATTLING AND BANGING ON DOOR)
GILBERT:	(V.O.) The position was dire. He couldn't possibly go out into the freezing street as he was and if he remained he would certainly be given into custody in the morning. He looked in vain for something to cover himself with. The hats and coats were locked away out of reach in the inner hall, He tried the carpet –
	(FRANTIC BREATHLESS TUGGINGS)
GILBERT:	(V.O.) but it was fitted securely to the floor and moreover a heavy sideboard stood upon it. There was only one ray of hope–
THEODORE:	Ah…
GILBERT:	(V.O.) There were twelve chairs in the room and each had draped over its back an antimacassar to protect the chair from spoiling. Antimacassars are small pieces of fabric so they would not

	cover much but twelve might be made to hide something –
	(MUCH SIGHING AND RUSTLING OF FABRIC.)
THEODORE:	(SIGHING) Well, I suppose they cover me after a fashion. But a gentleman walking through South Kensington at 3 a.m. dressed in nothing whatever but antimacassars with the snow two feet deep on the ground will be sure to attract attention. I might pretend that I was doing it for a wager but who would believe me?
	(THE CHATTERING OF TEETH)
GILBERT:	(V.O.) Theodore grew very cold indeed. And then salvation came. Theodore looked out of the window –
	(POLICEMAN WHISTLING "A policeman's lot is not a happy one.")
GILBERT:	(V.O.) A policeman just outside was wearily plodding through the snow. Theodore suddenly saw the only sure way out of his difficulties -
THEODORE:	(CALLING) Policeman – can I have a word?
POLICEMAN:	(FROM OUTSIDE) Anything wrong, sir?

THEODORE:	I – I have been committing a burglary in this house and should fell deeply obliged if you will kindly take me into custody.
POLICEMAN:	Nonsense, sir, you'd much better go to bed.
THEODORE:	There is nothing I should like better but I live in Lincoln's Inn and I have nothing on but antimacassars. I am frozen. (PLEADING) Please take me into custody.
POLICEMAN:	If you insist, sir.
THEODORE:	The street door's unlocked.
	(THE RATTLE OF HANDCUFFS)
GILBERT:	(V.O.) The worthy policeman listened to his story. Then he put his great coat over Theodore and lent him his own handcuffs. Within ten minutes Theodore was thawing himself in Walton Street police station.
THEODORE:	Ahhhh…
GILBERT:	(V.O.) Within ten days he was convicted at the Old Bailey.
FOREMAN:	Guilty, my lord, guilty!
GILBERT:	(V.O.) And within ten years Theodore returned from penal servitude.
	(MELANCHOLY ORGAN MUSIC IN THE DISTANCE.)
GILBERT:	(V.O.) His parents meanwhile had taken advantage of an offer from Her Majesty's Government

to go and colonise Australia. His beloved Belinda was now married to a society burglar with magnificent connections in the highest social circles. And Mr John Davis had gone to meet his Maker. Theodore visited his grave to confront his nemesis..

THEODORE: Oh wretched Designer of Dados, how happy my life might have been were it not for our encounter.

(FOOSTEPS APPROACHING. A DISCREET COUGH NEARBY.)

DAVIS: Good afternoon, Theodore.
GILBERT: (V.O.) Theodore turned with a start. There by his side stood Mr John Davis, very much as he'd last seen him – and very much alive.
THEODORE: But – but I don't understand. You're dead.
DAVIS: I beg to differ. John Davis, Designer of Dados, is dead. But I am not John Davis. I was in the process of effecting a robbery in his house when you were foolish enough to interrupt me.
THEODORE: Then you are –
DAVIS: Samuel 'Thumbscrew' McFidget alias Thomas 'Fingers' O'Flaherty alias John 'Many Faces' Smithers alias –

THEODORE:	You – you are the famous Samuel 'Thumbscrew McFidget alias - ?
DAVIS:	Indeed I am. There's no need to go through all the aliases.
THEODORE:	(INDIGNANTLY) But - you – you made a fool of me! You betrayed me to the police! You got me transported. You -
DAVIS:	Don't blame me, Theodore. Blame your own incompetence. Now - good afternoon to you – and good luck for your future career, you're going to need it.
	(THE FOOTSTEPS RETREAT.)
THEODORE:	(CALLING AFTER HIM) Come back here – you rogue – you villain – you cheat! You're a disgrace to our calling! You've given the profession of burglary a bad name. You've –
	(HIS VOICE FADES AWAY.)
GILBERT:	(V.O.) But there was no reply. The old man was gone. In the ensuing days Septimus recovered from his shock sufficiently to manage enough petty pilfering to keep body and soul together. But the spirit had gone from him. The principles upon which he had based his life were in ruins. Finally he realised –

(CROSSFADE TO TAVERN SOUNDS)

THEODORE: You know, when you came down it, it's a terrible thing but there really is no honour among thieves.

(FADE TO CLOSING MUSIC AND CREDITS.)

THE END

WIDE AWAKE

First broadcast on Radio 4 on 28th May 2003 with the following cast –

GILBERT	Jonathan Coy
HAROLD SYMPERSON	Richard Derrington
UNCLE SPARROW	Chris Emmett
AUNT SPARROW / BRIDGET	Joanna Wake
GEORGINA SPARROW	Julia Hills
JAMES SPARROW	Tom George
JOHN SPARROW	Jamie Chapman

The director was SUE WILSON

(GILBERT'S VOICE HEARD MUTTERING IN AN UNDERTONE:)

GILBERT: (V.O.) Then the blanketing tickles – you feel like mixed pickles – so terribly sharp is the pricking,
And you're hot and you're cross, and you tumble and toss till there's nothing 'twixt you and the ticking…

(A BRIGHT BLAST FROM ONE OF THE SULLIVAN OVERTURES. GILBERT CUT IT OFF:)

GILBERT: (V.O.) Ahem! This is Gilbert without Sullivan – remember? Thank you. (CLEARS THROAT) Today's original story by W.S. Gilbert – without the melodic interruptions of Sir Arthur Sullivan - is a cautionary tale entitled Wide Awake.

(SOMEONE STROLLING DOWN THE STREET WHISTLING.)

GILBERT: (V.O.) Harold Symperson was in most people's eyes a very fortunate fellow. At the outset of this story, that is, before the unfortunate experiences I am about to relate. Indeed Harold Symperson often said to himself –

HAROLD:	You know, I am a very fortunate fellow.

(CROSSFADE TO BARBER'S SHOP.)

GILBERT:	He even said it to his barber.
HAROLD:	You know, I do believe I am a very fortunate fellow.
BARBER:	(OBSEQUIOUSLY AS HE SNIPS AWAY) Indeed, sir.
HAROLD:	I mean, here I am in my late thirties, blessed with a strong constitution and – let's have no false modesty – considerably above average good looks.
BARBER:	Remarkably handsome, if I may so, sir.
HAROLD:	Of course you can! It's only the truth. And then, of course, there's my financial situation –
BARBER:	Indeed, sir.
HAROLD:	On the advice of my late father – well, of course, he wasn't my late father when he gave me this advice – I put the money I had received from my extremely rich aunt - when she became my late extremely rich aunt – into an annuity. The result?
BARBER:	I believe you live very comfortably –
HAROLD:	So I do.
BARBER:	(A TRACE OF BITTERNESS) Without, I believe, having done a day's work in your life.
HAROLD:	There's never been the need. And work isn't something you do for the pleasure of it, is it?

BARBER:	I'm afraid I've never had the luxury, sir.
HAROLD:	So, as I said, I am a very fortunate fellow. And I suppose there is only one thing that I need to complete my happiness and that is – marriage.
BARBER:	Not always an unmixed blessing, sir.
HAROLD:	But it is me we are talking of. Life has always bestowed its blessings upon me – and to be honest I think I am something of a catch. No point in being modest is there?
BARBER:	Obviously not for you, sir, no.
HAROLD:	After all, I've already taken the first move.
BARBER:	You've started to look for the fortunate girl, sir?
HAROLD:	No, no, before that. I've ensured my life for ten thousand pounds. Now there's something to get the girls interested, eh?

(THE HAIR CUTTING STOPS.)

BARBER:	Well, sir, what do you think?
HAROLD:	A little pomade and I shall be perfect, quite perfect.

(CROSSFADE TO FOOTSTEPS AND WHISTLING AGAIN)

GILBERT:	(V.O.) Mr Harold Symperson had only recently moved to the great metropolis from the

charming Somerset village in which he had been brought up by his late parents. To him the City was a place of magic and wonder. It was not going to stay that way for long.

(FOOTSTEPS UP GRAVEL PATH AND OPENING OF DOOR WITH KEY.)

HAROLD: (CALLING) Hello, I'm back.
GILBERT: (V.O.) On his arrival in London Harold had taken up residence with his only surviving relations – the Sparrow family. The Sparrow family consisted of Uncle Sparrow –
UNCLE: There you are, my boy!
GILBERT: (V.O.) Aunt Sparrow –
AUNT: Harold! Welcome home!
GILBERT: (V.O.) Their daughter Georgina –
GEORGINA: (TREMULOUSLY) Dearest Harold!
GILBERT: (V.O.) and Georgina's two horsey brothers James –
JAMES: I say!!!
GILBERT: (V.O.) and John –
JOHN: I say too!!!!!

(CROSSFADE TO SUPPER BEING EATEN)

GILBERT: (V.O.) The Sparrows had generously welcomed Harold into the bosom of the family. Uncle Sparrow was something

	in the City – not very much in the City it has to be said.
HAROLD:	Delicious supper, Aunt Sparrow.
AUNT:	Thank you, Harold.
UNCLE:	So how was your day, Harold?
HAROLD:	Jolly busy. I had my hair cut.
AUNT:	It looks lovely.
GEORGINA:	(TREMULOUSLY) Oh, it looks heavenly.
JAMES:	I say, Georgina !!!
JOHN:	I say too!!!
GILBERT:	(V.O.) But it has also to be said that the Sparrows' welcome was not entirely without its calculating side. Uncle Sparrow did not earn a great deal. His horsey sons who were even less significant somethings in the City earned even less. The money Harold gave as a contribution towards his keep was more than generous because he was not very worldly about money – and the Sparrows thought it best to leave his innocence untarnished. After all, was it not feathering the Sparrows' nest?
	(CROSSFADE TO THE PIANO BEING PLAYED BADLY.)
GILBERT:	(V.O.) And then, of course, there was Georgina.
	(GEORGINA STARTS TO SING "COME INTO THE

	GARDEN, MAUD" VERY BADLY.)
GILBERT:	(V.O.) Georgina was over thirty and unmarried. She was also – there is no polite way of saying this – bony, angular and acid. In the words of a distinguished comic lyricist of my acquaintance, she could very well pass for forty-three in the dark with a light behind her.
	(GEORGINA SINGS TUNELESSLY ON. AS THIS FADES:)
GILBERT:	(V.O.) Someone less innocent than Harold Symperson would not have talked so openly of his intention to marry to somebody so very clearly unmarried as Georgina.
	(CRACKLING LOG FIRE.)
GEORGINA:	(BREATHILY) Dearest Harold –
HAROLD:	Yes, Georgina –
GEORGINA:	This she you talk of –
HAROLD:	Which she?
GEORGINA:	The she who will be only yours.
HAROLD:	Oh, that she!
GEORGINA:	Does this she have a name?
HAROLD:	Not yet, no.
GEORGINA:	Ah dear mysterious Harold, this she will have a name one day soon, will she not?

HAROLD:	Well, it will be rather difficult if she doesn't have a name because I wouldn't know what to call her, would I?
GEORGINA:	Dearest Harold, what a tease you are!
HAROLD:	Look – Georgina – when I know her name, of course I'll let you know what it is.
GEORGINA:	You naughty, naughty man.
HAROLD:	The fact is – I don't want to hurry into anything. After all, it does seem to me that with my fortune and my good looks I am a very remarkable catch for any woman.
GEORGINA:	(HUNGRILY) You are, Harold, you are.
	(THE ROARING FIRE. THE CLINK OF GLASSES.)
GILBERT:	(V.O.) Later that night after the parents had retired to bed, James and John proposed –
JAMES:	A game of cribbage –
JOHN:	And some bottles of this excellent beer. -
GILBERT:	(V.O.) Georgina, of course, did not imbibe as that would have been most unladylike. But her brothers drank freely and insisted Harold did the same –
JAMES:	Have another one, Harry.
JOHN:	Come on, Hal, don't be shy.
JAMES:	Cheers!
JOHN and HAROLD:	Cheers!

124

	(CROSSFADE TO GREATER CLINKING OF GLASSES.)
GILBERT:	(V.O.) Time passed. The game of cribbage began for the gentleman to take a second place to sampling more of the excellent beer.
JAMES:	Drink up, Harry, old chap!
JOHN:	Put hairs on your chest, Haroldy.
JOHN and JAMES:	Cheers!
HAROLD:	(FEEBLY) Cheers!!!
	(CROSSFADE TO FURTHER CLINKING OF GLASSES)
GILBERT:	(V.O.) The fact of the matter is that Harold Symperson had rarely imbibed before and had little or no capacity to – as the phrase goes – hold his liquor. Georgina was, of course, stone cold sober although strangely silent as the evening progressed. Her two brothers meanwhile matched Harold drink for drink without sustaining any visible inebriation.
JAMES:	Come on, Harry, no holding back.
JOHN:	Plenty more where that came from!
JAMES:	Cheers!
JOHN:	Cheers!
HAROLD:	(FAR GONE) Cheers – John. Cheers – James. Cheers – Georgina. I – you know I think I really ought to –

	(A GROAN AND A BODY FALLING TO THE FLOOR.)
GILBERT:	(V.O.) At that point Mr Harold Symperson slipped from his chair and into oblivion.
	(CROSSFADE TO HAROLD GROANING.)
HAROLD:	Ohhhhhhh!!!!
GILBERT:	(V.O.) The next morning Harold Symperson woke up to a new sensation in his life. He felt dreadful.
HAROLD:	Ohhhhhhhhhhh!!!!
GILBERT:	(V.O.) Spiders crawled across his eyes, snails crawled through his insides and heavy hammers assailed his ears. You probably know the feeling yourself.
HAROLD:	Ohhhhhhhhhhhhhhh!!!!!
	(A VOICE HEARD CALLING FROM BELOW.)
GEORGINA:	Harold! Harold! It's breakfast time.
HAROLD:	Ohhhh!
GEORGINA:	Harold!
HAROLD:	(DEEP BREATH) Oh, very well.
	(FEET DESCENDING THE STAIRCASE. DOOR OPENS TO RATTLE OF BREAKFAST THINGS.)

UNCLE:	(VERY WELCOMING) Ah, Harold, dear boy, come in, take a seat. There's one there - by Georgina, of course.
AUNT:	Do help yourself to whatever you need, won't you, Harold, dear?
	(THE CONTINUING NOISE OF BREAKFAST.)
GILBERT:	(V.O.) Through his mental haze, Harold became aware that everybody seemed to be smiling very broadly. Georgina in particular smiled at him with a warmth which would have been charming in somebody with better teeth. Something, he decided was in the air.
	(BREAKFAST NOISES THEN FINALLY:)
UNCLE:	(CLEARING THROAT) Well, I must say this is wonderful news, Harold.
HAROLD:	I'm sorry, uncle, what is wonderful news?
UNCLE:	The news of your engagement.
HAROLD:	My what?
UNCLE:	Your engagement.
HAROLD:	I – I wasn't aware that I was engaged.
UNCLE:	Now, now, Harold, don't go coy on us. We're all party to your little secret.
HAROLD:	I don't have a little secret.

UNCLE:	Oh, I think you do. Or rather – you and Georgina share a little secret, don't you, Georgina?
GEORGINA:	Indeed, papa.
HAROLD:	Then maybe Georgina can tell us what that secret is.
JAMES:	That's not very proper.
JOHN:	It's supposed to be the fellow who does it.
HAROLD;	Does what?
JAMES:	Announces the engagement. You fool!
JOHN:	Oaf!
GEORGINA:	Now, now. James, John, don't get cross at a happy time like this. <u>(PAUSE)</u> Harold, last night, you asked me to be your wife.
HAROLD:	I did what?
GEORGINA:	And – after a seemly display of maidenly reluctance – I have agreed to be your bride.
HAROLD:	But – but I don't remember any of this.
GEORGINA:	Do not tease so, Harold. I can remember every loving word of your proposal.
JAMES:	Me too.
JOHN:	And me. Especially the bit about wanting Georgina to share your wealth –
JAMES:	And claim on the insurance if you ever kicked the bucket.
HAROLD:	You're all sure this happened?
GEORGINA:	No doubt of it.
UNCLE:	And to save you the bother of asking me for Georgina's hand in marriage, I'll let you know

	straight away that I willingly give my consent.
AUNT:	So do I.
JAMES and JOHN:	And so do we.
GILBERT:	(V.O.) Harold Symperson had just experienced the first truly unpleasant surprise of his sheltered life. Georgina was so very convincing and her two brothers were both so very convinced – as well as both being very big and strong – that Harold saw no alternative. After all, he had no recollection of anything.
HAROLD:	(FAINTLY) Very well, if you all say so, then we must be engaged.

(A CHEER FROM THE FAMILY)

UNCLE:	Go on, Harold, kiss your bride to be.
HAROLD:	Well, if you don't mind, I'd –
UNCLE:	We don't mind at all. Go on – kiss her.

(A PAUSE FOLLOWED BY A VERY TENTATIVE KISS. THE FAMILY CHEER AGAIN.)

GILBERT:	(V.O.) Over the next few weeks Harold tried several ways of evading his forthcoming fate.
HAROLD:	Georgina – do you not think we are a little young for marriage?

GEORGINA: Young! Oh, God bless you, Harold.

(A SMACKING KISS. CROSSFADE TO:)

HAROLD: James – John – what would you think if I went away on a little holiday for a few days just to –

JAMES: No holiday before the honeymoon.

JOHN: I mean to say, Harry, we're not violent fellows. Well, I'm not. James does have a vicious streak. But I think you can imagine what we might do if you tried to wriggle out of marrying Georgina.

JAMES: Perhaps better not imagine it actually. Because it might be awfully violent and unpleasant.

JOHN: Involving cricket bats –
JAMES: And horse whips –
JOHN: And fly whisks –

(THEY GIVE A SINISTER HORSEY CHUCKLE) (CROSSFADE TO FEET WALKING THE STREETS. BUT NOW HAROLD HUMS A DEAD MARCH.)

GILBERT: (V.O.) Harold Symperson was well and truly trapped. His plans for future happiness lay in ruins. He had no illusions – he did not love Georgina and could only assume the beer had persuaded

130

	him he did. And now at his lowest ebb he secretly dreamed of someone to love.
	(HE BUMPS INTO SOMEBODY)
HAROLD:	I'm most terribly sorry, madam.
BRIDGET:	It was my fault as well.
GILBERT:	(V.O.) Facing Harold was a plump and rosy lady of middle years. There was something about her he found very pleasing.
	(ROMANTIC VICTORIAN MUSIC WELLS UP.)
HAROLD:	Perhaps, madam, you will allow me to accompany you home to – to ensure that you have sustained no injury from our unfortunate physical encounter.
BRIDGET:	That is most kind of you, sir. I do not live very far from here. In fact, in Great Coram Street.
HAROLD:	Then let us proceed there. My name is Harold – Harold Symperson.
BRIDGET:	And I am Bridget – Bridget Comfit.
HAROLD:	You – you are married?
BRIDGET:	Alas, Mr Symperson, my dear husband died some years ago. I am a widow.
HAROLD:	Perfect.

(TWO SETS OF FEET WALKING THROUGH THE STREET. THE ROMANTIC MUSIC WELLS UP.)

GILBERT: (V.O.) Bridget Comfit was not only comely and a widow, she also possessed a reasonable private income and a very cosy little house in Great Coram Street. She had no children and no visible dependants. She was in every way an ideal partner. By the end of the walk home, Harold Symperson was entranced. Strangely he did not mention that he was engaged to be married to someone else.

(QUACKING OF DUCKS ON POND.)

BRIDGET: Here, ducklings, here!

HAROLD: Are they not delightful?

GILBERT: (V.O.) Bridget and Harold met on a fairly regular basis for simple pleasures like walking and feeding the ducks. Somehow or other enough guile had entered Harold Symperson's soul for him to successfully keep these meetings from the Sparrows.

(ROMANTIC MUSIC BUILDS UP AGAIN. ACCOMPANIED BY QUACKING DUCKS.)

GILBERT:	(V.O.) And then one morning by the duck pond Harold felt an urgent question welling up from the depth of his soul.
HAROLD:	Bridget – will you marry me?
BRIDGET:	Oh yes, Harold, of course.
	(ROMANTIC MUSIC CUTS OFF ABRUPTLY)
GILBERT:	(V.O.) There was, of course, only one problem. Harold Symperson was already engaged to Georgina Sparrow. The problem became more acute when Harold made actual plans to wed Bridget Comfit on a certain Tuesday in December at St. Pancras Church, Euston Square. This event, he felt, would not be appreciated by either Georgina, her parents – or by her two very violent and impulsive brothers. So despite a natural truthfulness he thought it best not to mention it. This was, he reflected, acting rather an underhand part towards Georgina but what was to be done?
	(SOUNDS OF DISTURBED SLEEP, NIGHTMARES.)
HAROLD:	Ohhhh! Noooo!!!
GILBERT:	(V.O.) The night before his planned wedding Harold Symperson slept ill. It seemed

HAROLD:	that Georgina and Uncle Sparrow and all the other Sparrows rose up to accuse him. (IN HIS SLEEP) Pray, Georgina, don't look at me in that way… Georgina…
	(CROSSFADE TO DAWN CHORUS.)
GILBERT:	(V.O.) But in the morning his doubts vanished. It seemed to him the most natural thing in the world that a man who had engaged himself to Georgina should take the earliest opportunity of getting out of the engagement.
	(THE SOUNDS OF BREAKFAST IN BED.)
GILBERT:	(V.O.) Nevertheless, Harold pleaded a bad bilious headache and took his breakfast in bed. Somehow he couldn't face the family. He remained there until Uncle Sparrow and his two sons had started for the City.
	(A DISTANT FRONT DOOR SLAMS)
HAROLD:	There they go! Quarter to ten on the dot!
GILBERT:	(V.O.) At ten o'clock he knew Aunt Sparrow and Georgina would go down to the kitchen to

	have their daily row over the cook's accounts. He quickly dressed and made his way downstairs –
	(TIPTOING DOWN A FLIGHT OF STAIRS.)
GILBERT:	(V.O.) He reached the ground floor – safely – kissed a last farewell to Georgina's very long galoshes in the umbrella-stand – (A QUICK KISS)
GILBERT:	(V.O.) then crept out shutting the front door quietly behind him –
	(DOOR QUIETLY CLOSED. CROSSFADE TO BUSY STREETS.)
GILBERT:	(V.O.) There was time to spare before Bridget would arrive at the church so Harold spent part of it in walking round Euston Square – which can be done in two thousand one hundred paces. But still in plenty of time he entered the church –
	(FADE STREET SOUNDS AS MASSIVE CHURCH DOOR CREAKS OPEN. FOOTSTEPS ACROSS STONE FLOORS.)

GILBERT:	(V.O.) There was no one there but the beadle who asked if he could be of any assistance.
HAROLD:	Yes, I think maybe you can. I'm on the early side. But you see – the fact is - I've come here to be married.
JAMES:	(SUDDENLY) Have you now?
JOHN:	I say!
GILBERT:	(V.O.) Harold found himself clapped on the back by Georgina's two headstrong brothers – and their father.
UNCLE:	We wondered what you were up to. We were paying a visit to a money-lender in Euston Square and watched you walking round and round the square.
JAMES:	So we got curious –
JOHN:	And we followed you.
UNCLE:	So, sir, you've come here to be married, have you?
JAMES:	Fire and fury!
JOHN:	Zounds and the devil!
GILBERT:	(V.O.) This was, Harold reflected, one of the most tremendously dramatic situations in Modern History. But what was he to do?
UNCLE:	Say something, you rogue!
JAMES:	Speak up –
JOHN:	Or take the consequences.
GILBERT:	(V.O.) At this potentially fatal moment, Harold was fortunate to have a moment of inspiration such as only comes to man at rare points in his life. He gave a sudden start, rolled his eyes, and gasped –

(MUCH COD GASPING.)

HAROLD: Where – where am I?
JAMES: You're in a bloody church!
JOHN: Waiting to get bloody married!
HAROLD: But how did I come here?
JAMES: On your bloody feet – how else?
HAROLD: But I don't remember anything about it! The last thing I remember is being in bed with a bilious headache and trying to go to sleep. And here I am – dressed and wide-awake – in St Pancras Church. What is the inference?
JOHN: That you're a bounder!
JAMES: A scoundrel!
UNCLE: A disgrace to the family!
HAROLD: My dear uncle, my good – but violent – cousins, this is very distressing to me for I thought I had quite shaken it off.
UNCLE: Shaken what off exactly?
HAROLD: Well, you see it must be years since I've done such a thing as walk in my sleep.
JAMES: I'll say!
JOHN: I'll say too!
HAROLD: You see back in my early years I once remained in a state of somnambulism for nearly a week. It really is most providential that you happened to be here.
UNCLE: (DRYLY) You could say that.
HAROLD: Though perhaps another time it would be better not to wake me quite so suddenly. It's very

	dangerous to wake a somnambulist with a violent shock. Better let him have his sleep out.
UNCLE:	We'll bear that in mind, won't we boys?
JAMES and JOHN:	I'll say!
UNCLE:	So what do you propose to do now?
HAROLD:	I – I think the best thing I can do is go home and got to bed again, don't you?
UNCLE:	Good idea! You take one arm, James, and you take the other, John.
JOHN and JAMES:	Very good, pater.

(CROSSFADE TO FOOTSTEPS ON STREET.)

GILBERT: (V.O.) So they marched him home with Uncle Sparrow walking behind, keeping the ferrule of his walking-stick in the small of Harold's back.

(THE RESTLESS RUSTLING OF BEDSHEETS.)

GILBERT: (V.O.) Harold immediately took to his bed again, trying to make the best of his disappointment.

HAROLD: I feel very sorry for Bridget but what could a fellow do? I'll be able to send her an explanation of what's happened and put things right once things have settled down. After all, it'll only delay our happiness for a few

	days. And I have to say, Harold Symperson, you do deserve something of a pat on the back for your quick-thinking. That was a difficulty which would have overwhelmed ninety-nine out of a hundred but razor sharp I came up with an explanation – and they bought it!
GILBERT:	(V.O.) By the next morning Harold was feeling in much better spirits – and also very peckish. So he went and joined the family for breakfast.
	(DOOR OPENING. THE RATTLE OF BREAKFAST THINGS.)
HAROLD:	Good morning!
	(SUDDENLY THE BREAKFAST NOISES CEASE.)
HAROLD:	Yes, good morning, uncle! How are you, dear aunt? Ha, John! Ha, James! Georgina, my love, good morning.
GILBERT:	(V.O.) The Sparrow family exchanged significant glances but made no response to Harold's greeting.
HAROLD:	And a very lovely morning it is too if I may say so. The sort of morning that makes you glad to be alive.

GILBERT:	(V.O.) Still there was no response but Uncle Sparrow turned to Aunt Sparrow.
UNCLE:	(SOFTLY) He's at it again!
AUNT:	(SOFTER STILL) Hush, don't speak so loud. You'll wake him.
GEORGINA:	(SOFTER STILL) Poor Harold, his eyes are open and yet he's evidently fast asleep.
UNCLE:	That is always the case with somnambulists. The sleeping brain receives its impressions through the eyes, nose and ears.
JAMES:	His nose and ears are wide open also.
JOHN:	So they were yesterday.
HAROLD:	Excuse me – what is going on here?
UNCLE:	There's a famous case of somnambulism I heard about in Italy. A girl was found in suspicious circumstances in the bedroom of an Italian nobleman and the most unfavourable inferences were drawn as to her moral character. But fortunately she was spotted crossing a most dangerous plank over a watermill in her petticoat singing the most complex melodies at the top of her voice. She proved to be a confirmed somnambulist too.
AUNT:	Extraordinary, dear.
GEORGINA:	The wonders of the human brain!
HAROLD:	Excuse me – am I to suppose that you are under the impression that I am asleep?

GEORGINA: You know, except that his utterance is thick, there is really very little difference between his sleeping and waking voice.

UNCLE: You are right, Georgina, Though I fancy his coloratura will not have much to recommend it.

HAROLD: (GETTING CROSS) Look, if this is some sort of joke then I've had quite enough of it. I'm hungry and I want some breakfast.

(HAROLD GRASPS SOME BREAKFAST THINGS. A STRUGGLE.)

AUNT: Quick, take his knife away, Georgina.

GEORGINA: Yes, mamma.

AUNT: And James, cut up his bacon –
JAMES: Yes, mamma.
AUNT: Let him eat it with a tea-spoon.
HAROLD: But this is preposterous. You can't eat fried bacon with a tea-spoon so as to enjoy it.

(A FURTHER STRUGGLE OVER CUTLERY)

UNCLE: I'm afraid I must insist on his knife being removed. In his current somnambulistic state he has no control over what he is doing. John and James, sit on either side of him and watch his movement most carefully.

JOHN and JAMES:	Right you are, papa.
	(A RE-ARRANGEMENT OF CHAIRS. THE CLANK OF BREAKFAST CUTLERY AS APPROPRIATE.)
HAROLD:	This is absurd! Uncle – I appeal to you.
UNCLE:	Now remember everybody you must be very careful not to wake him as that would be most dangerous. As he told us himself, these trances usually last a week.
HAROLD:	But I'm not in a trance!
UNCLE:	John, feed him with a spoon.
JOHN:	Yes, papa.
HAROLD:	But, uncle –
UNCLE:	James, hold his tea cup and give him a sip occasionally.
HAROLD:	Uncle, I beg – I <u>beg</u> that you will allow me to have my breakfast in peace.
UNCLE:	Now give him a bit of muffin, James. A tiny morsel will suffice.
HAROLD:	Uncle, I had nothing to eat yesterday on account of my bilious headache and I am literally starving.
UNCLE:	Now a spoonful of egg, John. Not too much mind.
HAROLD:	(HALF CHOKING) Thank you but I can feed myself. I want no assistance from anyone. Indeed, I am quite, quite awake!

	(A SLIGHT PAUSE. THEN:)
UNCLE:	Now a mouthful of tea – but be careful – it's running down his waistcoat.
GILBERT:	(V.O.) There was nothing for it but to submit to be fed by the hulking brothers. But it didn't end there. The two brothers devoted themselves to taking care of him with the extraordinary assiduity. They took him out for a walk every day –
	(FOOTSTEPS IN STREET)
HAROLD:	Look – James – John – a joke's a joke but this has been going on for days now.
JAMES:	(SOTTO VOCE) Extraordinary, eh, John?
JOHN:	(DITTO) I'll say! Who'd have thought it? You'd never guess he was in a trance if you didn't know it.
HAROLD:	Perhaps if we went this way, I could –
JAMES:	Look out, John, the fellow's wandering off.
JOHN:	Can't have that now, can we? This way now.
	(CLATTER OF FOOD)

GILBERT:	V.O.) They fed him carefully at mealtimes.
JAMES:	Small bit of meat –
JOHN:	Fragment of potato –
JAMES:	Morsel of cabbage –
HAROLD:	Please let me eat for myself –
JOHN:	Did you hear that, James?
JAMES:	You'd swear he wasn't asleep.

(CROSSFADE TO BEDROOM ACCOUSTIC)

JAMES:	Jacket –
JOHN;	Necktie –
JAMES:	Waistcoat –
JOHN:	Shoes –
GILBERT:	(V.O.) They also undressed him and put him to bed at night –
JAMES:	Shoes –
JOHN;	Waistcoat –
JAMES:	Necktie –
JOHN:	Jacket –
GILBERT:	(V.O.) And dressed him again the next morning. This went on for several days. His unfortunate condition was explained to all visitors who took a deep interest in watching his movements. And indeed all of them agreed there was something very unusual in his appearance and demeanour.

(SOUND OF LETTERS BEING OPENED)

GILBERT: (V.O.) Uncle Sparrow opened all his letters –

UNCLE: (READING) Ahhh… Hmm… Very interesting.

AUNT: (ALSO READING) Indeed… Mmmm

HAROLD: Uncle, that is my personal correspondence.

UNCLE: Julia, I do believe he's talking in his sleep again.

AUNT: Hush, dear, or we'll wake him.

UNCLE: I really think I shall have to take charge of all this correspondence until he is in a condition to take care of it himself.

AUNT: I agree, dear.

HAROLD: I protest, I protest.

(ANOTHER LETTER OPENED)

UNCLE: (READING IT) Now this letter, Julia, is exceptionally interesting. It comes from a Mrs Bridget Comfit.

HAROLD: (AGITATED) Bridget! Dear Bridget!

AUNT: Go on, dear. Pray take no notice of him.

UNCLE: Mrs Comfit expresses some dismay that Harold did not appear at St Pancras Church at the expected hour for their wedding. She apparently waited for a considerable time at the

	church before realising that she had been heartlessly abandoned. She indicates that she wishes to have nothing further to do with him.
HAROLD:	Let me see that – please.
AUNT:	Definitely one for you to take care of, dear.
HAROLD:	(FINALLY LOSING IT) No, this is intolerable. I know you're paying me out for the deception I practised on you at the church. I suppose it's only right that I should suffer some little mortification for that trick but enough is enough! Unless you give me at once an assurance in writing signed by the whole family that I am as wide awake as you all are then I shall appeal for protection to the laws of the land. I'm not quite sure under which Act of Parliament my grievance would come but I intend to find out – unless you all instantly cease this charade.
	(PAUSE)
AUNT:	(QUIETLY) I think he's still in that trance, dear.
UNCLE:	Best leave him to it.
	(A DOOR SHUT. HAROLD GIVES A CRY OF EXASPERATION.) (CROSSFADE TO BREAKFAST NOISES.)

GILBERT:	(V.O.) But after some days of this ghastly ideal, Fate finally decreed that events would take a fresh turn.
	(ANOTHER LETTER BEING OPENED)
UNCLE:	Ah, another letter for dear Harold.
GEORGINA:	What does it say, papa?
JAMES:	It's good fun opening another fellow's correspondence.
JOHN:	I'll say.
HAROLD:	I think I'm going mad. Leave that letter alone!
UNCLE:	(READING) Now this really is most important. It is from the office where Harold it seems has insured his life for the benefit of his widow – whoever that may be – for the sum of £10,000.
GEORGINA:	Dear generous Harold was no doubt thinking of providing for me before – before his terrible affliction.
	(SHE STARTS TO WEEP FOR A FEW PERFUNCTORY MOMENTS.)
AUNT:	There, there, dear, I'm sure he'll come to his senses soon.
UNCLE:	Well, indeed, I very much hope so. For this letter informs Harold that the annual premium on his policy is still unpaid. It also states that the fourteen days of

	grace had expired and that unless the secretary receives a cheque for the full amount – namely three hundred and twenty pounds – in the course of the afternoon, the policy will, ipso facto, become null and void.
GEORGINA:	Oh, papa, how terrible.
JAMES:	I say!
JOHN:	Zounds and whiskers!
UNCLE:	(MATTER OF FACT) Harold, you had better attend to this at once. At once. I am surprised that you have neglected so important, so vital matter.
	(A RUSTLE AS THE LETTER IS HANDED OVER.)
GILBERT:	(V.O.) Harold Symperson, an innocent no longer, saw his advantage at a glance.
HAROLD:	I will gladly attend to this to-morrow, uncle, if I am in a condition to do so.
UNCLE:	But to-morrow won't do. The secretary says expressly that the money must be paid this afternoon.
GEORGINA:	My dear Harold, pray do not risk a delay. The matter is of the highest moment. Please be good enough to write a cheque at once.
HAROLD:	I will write a cheque for the amount as soon as I am awake. But these trances usually last a week.

UNCLE:	Come, come, the joke has been carried far enough. We were only chaffing you, weren't we?
	(THE REST OF THE FAMILY AGREES.)
UNCLE:	So come along and write the cheque at once. Please.
HAROLD:	Uncle Sparrow, Aunt Sparrow, Georgina, John and James – you have done your best to persuade me that I have been in a somnambulistic trance for three days. At first I doubted it but it has become impossible to reject the evidence of so many disinterested witnesses. I am now quite convinced that you were right and I am wrong. I am, no doubt, fast asleep.
	(THE FAMILY STARTS TO PROTEST BUT HAROLD OVER-RIDES THEM.)
HAROLD:	I am very much obliged to you all for the great care and attention you have bestowed on me in this unfortunate and abnormal condition. It is not likely to last above three or four days longer and as soon as I am thoroughly awake and capable of attending to business, I will certainly send a cheque for my premium. But not till then.

	(MORE PROTESTS FROM THE FAMILY)
UNCLE:	Harold, I admit to you the whole thing has been a joke. But as you said yourself there comes a time when all this fooling must come to an end. Write the cheque like a good fellow or Georgina will be left penniless.
	(THE FAMILY ROAR AGREEMENT)
GEORGINA:	My own, my love, please don't be ridiculous. You are older than I and in the natural course of events I shall survive you. If the cheque is not written at once, I shall be a penniless widow!
	(MORE AGREEMENT FROM THE FAMILY)
HAROLD:	Georgina, I promise that I will write this cheque –
GEORGINA:	My own!
HAROLD:	When I am awake. After all a cheque written in a state of somnambulism is going to be invalid.
	(GROANS OF DESPAIR FROM THE FAMILY.)
GILBERT:	(V.O.) The whole family went down on their knees to him –
ALL:	(ON KNEES) Please!

GILBERT: (V.O.) But Harold stuck to his colours.

(SOUND OF BREATHLESS RUNNING.)

GILBERT: (V.O.) The hours crept on. It was three o'clock and the office closed at four. Finding nothing would shake Harold's resolution, Uncle Sparrow rushed out to his bankers with the family plate, Aunt Sparrow's jewels, and a bundle of American stock.

(THE BREATHING STOPS WITH THIS HEAVY LOAD BEING DROPPED ON A COUNTER.)
(A SLIGHT PAUSE THEN THE BREATHLESS RUNNING CONTINUES AGAIN.)

GILBERT: (V.O.) Uncle Sparrow borrowed the three hundred and twenty pounds on the security – and paid the premium five minutes before the office closed.

(AGAIN THE BREATHLESS RUNNING ENDS IN A HEAVY LOAD BEING DROPPED ON A COUNTER.)
(CROSSFADE TO BREAKFAST THINGS.)

GILBERT:	(V.O.) The next morning, Harold came down to breakfast wide awake.
	(DOOR OPENING)
HAROLD:	Good morning, aunt, uncle, cousin Georgina, cousin James and cousin John.
UNCLE:	How are you feeling, dear boy?
HAROLD:	Very wide awake. I think you'll agree I seem wide awake, won't you?
	(THE FAMILY ALL AGREES.)
UNCLE:	Yes, yes, we're all delighted to see you recovered. And as you are now no longer fast asleep perhaps you would be kind enough to favour me at once with a cheque for three hundred and twenty pounds.
HAROLD:	Why should I do that, uncle?
UNCLE:	It's the amount of your insurance premium.
HAROLD:	What insurance premium?
GEORGINA:	The one that provides for your widow in the event of your death.
HAROLD:	Oh, that premium!
UNCLE:	What do you mean?
HAROLD:	Uncle, I'm really surprised that you've taken upon yourself to pay the premium on a policy which I have no intention of keeping up.

UNCLE:	What?
HAROLD:	I was asleep all the time – remember? I altogether decline to hold myself responsible. If you wish to squander three hundred and twenty pounds on a pointless policy that is your affair.
UNCLE:	What!!!
GEORGINA:	Papa!
UNCLE:	You refuse to pay?
HAROLD:	Absolutely.

(A HUGE ROW ENSUES WITH ALL THE FAMILY ARGUING AT ONCE AND GEORGINA IN HYSTERICS.)

GILBERT: (V.O.) An angry scene ensued which resulted in the final rupture of Harold Symperson's engagement with Georgina Sparrow -

(A BIG KISS)

BRIDGET:	My own!
HAROLD:	My dove!
GILBERT:	(V.O.) And the resumption of his engagement with Mrs Bridget Comfit.

(WEDDING MARCH.)

GILBERT: (V.O.) They planned a quiet wedding ceremony. At least Harold planned a quiet ceremony. When they got there, the church was packed.

(OVER WEDDING MARCH, A CONVERSATION IN WHISPERS.)

HAROLD:	Bridget, who are these people?
BRIDGET:	Just members of my family?
HAROLD:	But you're a widow with no children.
BRIDGET:	Yes, but I do have seven brothers and three sisters with all their children. Then there's my three uncles, two aunts and all my cousins. And –
HAROLD:	You never mentioned them before.
BRIDGET:	(MOCK SURPRISE) Didn't I? Well, they're all longing to meet you. Several of my brothers and all my uncles have the most wonderful schemes for how you can invest all that money of yours which is sitting around doing nothing.
HAROLD:	But –
BRIDGET;	Harold, the vicar is waiting. You can hear all about their plans afterwards. (PAUSE) Harold? (PAUSE) Harold – come back!

(THE SOUND OF HAROLD RETREATING FOOTSTEPS DOWN THE AISLE TO SHOCKED REACTIONS.)

HAROLD: (AS HE RUNS) Let me out of here!

GILBERT: (V.0.) Which just goes to prove - you can never be too wide-awake. Things are seldom what they seem. Skim milk masquerades as cream. Highlows pass as patent leathers. Jackdaws strut in peacock's feathers….

(THE MUSIC OF LITTLE BUTTERCUP AND THE CAPTAIN'S DUET – FROM WHICH THESE WORDS COME – FROM ACT TWO OF **H.M.S. PINAFORE** HAS STARTED UP BENEATH HIS SPEECH. SUDDENLY IN HORROR GILBERT REALISES WHAT IS HAPPENING.)

GILBERT: No – no – No Sullivan! No Sullivan! Stop! Stop!

(HIS PROTESTS ARE DROWNED BY THE PLAYOUT MUSIC)

THE END

MR FOSTER'S GOOD FAIRY

First broadcast on Radio 4 on 4th June 2003 with the following cast –

GILBERT	Jonathan Coy
CYRIL FOSTER	Ian Brooker
FAIRY / LADY FOSTER	Sara Coward
JAKE / LORD PORTICO	Lennox Greaves
SAMUEL / MR BORTLE	David Bannerman

The director was SUE WILSON

	(GILBERT'S VOICE HEARD MUTTERING IN AN UNDERTONE:)
GILBERT:	(V.O.) Then the bedclothes all creep to the ground in a heap, and you pick 'em all up in a tangle; Next your pillow resigns and politely declines to remain at its usual angle!
	(A BRIGHT BLAST FROM ONE OF THE SULLIVAN OVERTURES. GILBERT CUTS IT OFF:)
GILBERT:	(V.O.) Excuse me! This is Gilbert without Sullivan. (MUSIC QUICKLY RETURNS) No tricks now! All Gilbert – no Sullivan. (MUSIC STOPS) Thank you. (CLEARING HIS THROAT) Ahem! Today's story by W.S.Gilbert unencumbered by the crotchets and quavers of Sir Arthur Sullivan is entitled – Mr Foster's Good Fairy.
	(FOSTER – EARLY THIRTIES - HUMMING CHEERFULLY AS HE SERVES IN HIS SHOP.)
FOSTER:	Three-penn'orth of chocolate cream, madam. And a Bath bun? Very good, ma'am.

GILBERT:	(V.O.) Mr Foster was a confectioner on a small scale in the Borough Road in South East London.
FOSTER:	A penny ice, little lady? My pleasure.
GILBERT:	(V.O.) Mr Foster was happily married to Louisa and they had two fine young children.
FOSTER:	Bath buns, sir? Three did you say?
GILBERT:	(V.O.) Mr Foster's life seemed remarkably quiet and ordinary. But the fact is that his career had been somewhat of a chequered one and his ups and downs had been many.
FOSTER:	Oh yes, I can most definitely recommend our humbugs!
GILBERT:	(V.O.) Not to put too fine a point on it Mr Foster carried not one but quite a fine selection of guilty secrets. It is on this fact that our eminently logical and factual story hinges.
	(SHOP BELL GOES AS DOOR OPENS.)
SERGEANT:	(DEEP SCOTTISH VOICE) Good morning – and a happy new year!
FOSTER:	(APPEARING) And good morning to you, sir, and a happy new – (HE GRINDS TO A HALT) Can I – can I –
	(HE COLLAPSES INTO SHOCKED SILENCE.)

GILBERT:	(V.O.) Mr Foster gasped in horror. It was the second of January. Standing in front of him was a sergeant of Highlanders in full uniform. The sight sent shivers down his spine.
SERGEANT:	I'm sorry – did I startle you?
FOSTER:	(IN A PANIC) No – no – not at all. How – how can I help you?
SERGEANT:	Do you stock acidulated drops?
FOSTER:	Acid drops? Did you say – acid drops?
SERGEANT:	I did. (PAUSE) You are a confectioner, aren't you?
FOSTER:	Yes, of course. That's what it says on the front of the shop, I believe. Now let me see – do we have acid drops? Yes, we do. We do. Any reason why you wanted to know?
SERGEANT:	I thought I might buy two penn'orth.
FOSTER:	Oh yes, of course, what a good idea. Two penn'orth coming up.
	(THE RATTLE OF JARS AS FOSTER NERVOUSLY SERVES OUT THE ACID DROPS. OVER THIS:)
GILBERT:	(V.O.) Something about the sergeant's stare threw Mr Foster into a complete panic. He was convinced he had been recognised and his past was catching up with him. He could

	not wait to get the sergeant out of the shop.
FOSTER:	There, sir, acidulated drops. That'll be er –
SERGEANT:	Tuppence.
FOSTER:	Exactly, sir. Very funny, ha ha ha.

(THE CLINK OF MONEY)

FOSTER:	Thank you, sir, thank you. You're most kind. It's a pleasure to do business with you.
SERGEANT:	(PUZZLED) I'm not sure I can say the same. This is one of the strangest shops I've ever set foot in.
FOSTER:	Ha, ha, ha, very kind of you to say so, sir. And a very good day to you. Lovely weather for the time of year too, eh?
SERGEANT:	I think you'll find it's snowing.

(HE OPENS THE DOOR. A HOWLING GALE. THEN THE DOOR IS SHUT AND SILENCE RETURNS.)

FOSTER:	(WHIMPERING) Oh – dash it – dash it all – he knows me. I know he knows me. He knows I know he knows me. I know that he knows that I know that he knows me. I shall be dragged away from the bosom of my family and I - I shall be tried for desertion.

	(A WAIL OF DESPAIR. FOLLOWED BY A MAGUC PING!)
GILBERT:	(V.O.) At this point something truly extraordinary happened. Almost as if Mr Foster was in a dream. For he heard quite distinctly a pipy little voice.
FAIRY:	(SOFTLY) Cheer up, Mr Foster!
FOSTER:	(STARTLED) What was that?
FAIRY:	I said – cheer up, Mr Foster!
FOSTER:	Yes, I know, but where are you?
FAIRY:	Over here.
GILBERT:	(V.O.) Mr Foster looked round and could see nobody. For a brief moment he actually thought he was going mad.
FAIRY:	I said – over here.
GILBERT:	(V.O.) At last Mr Foster's eye came to rest on a small twelfth-cake – all decorated and iced in preparation for Twelfth Night. On it stood a small plaster-of-Paris fairy.
FOSTER:	But you're a cake decoration, you can't –
FAIRY:	Oh yes, I can!
GILBERT:	(V.O.) And the fairy hopped off her box of sugar-plums and picked her way carefully through the tracery that decorated the surface of the cake. Mr Foster watched in amazement.
FOSTER:	I – I've never seen anything like this before.
FAIRY:	Not many people have.

	(A DAINTY LITTLE SHRIEK.)
GILBERT:	(V.O.) The fairy tumbled over a plaster-of-Paris ship decoration but regained her balance and reached the edge of the cake.
FAIRY:	I'm afraid, Mr Foster, that it's too high for me to jump off this cake. And if I try to scramble down I shall tear my clothes. I would therefore be most grateful if you would kindly let me step on to your hand.
FOSTER:	(GALLANTLY) Yes, yes, of course. Allow me.
GILBERT:	(V.O.) The fairy stepped daintily on his hand where she looked up at him sympathetically.
FAIRY:	Something is troubling you, Mr Foster.
FOSTER:	Yes, it is, miss – er ma'am. (PAUSE) I'm not quite sure how I'm supposed to address a fairy.
FAIRY:	It's a common problem. But I have no objection to being addressed as 'miss'.
FOSTER:	Then 'miss' I shall call you, miss. You see I don't meet many fairies in my line of business.
FAIRY:	You can't possibly know that, Mr Foster. We fairies get everywhere. Now what exactly is your problem?
FOSTER:	I have a guilty past and because of my guilty past I am about to

FAIRY: be plucked from the arms of my loving Louisa.

FAIRY: That would be a great tragedy. Particularly since from my observation she isn't much of a businesswoman. She gives sweets away to children for nothing.

FOSTER: Mrs Foster is all heart. Besides, she is a born lady and can't bear the idea of selling anything.

FAIRY: (A DELICATE COUGH) I think you had better tell me your history and explain your predicament.

FOSTER: It's a long story.

FAIRY: I'm not going anywhere.

FOSTER: Well, you see, I wasn't born a confectioner. I was born into a highly respectable family and after nineteen years of remarkable and exceptional ordinariness I became a Government clerk in the Bitter Beer branch of the Malt and Hops Department of the Inland Revenue Office.

FAIRY: Where no doubt you prospered?

FOSTER: After a fashion. You see I invented a wholly new system of cooking accounts.

FAIRY: Which your Heads of Department approved of?

FOSTER: Not exactly. In fact they took rather a dim view of my behaviour. Instead of praising my ingenuity, these blinkered men threatened to call in the

FAIRY:	police if I didn't make my excuses and resign immediately. Which, as a man of honour, you did?
FOSTER:	Well, I didn't stay around to discuss the matter. Finding myself penniless I enlisted in a regiment of Highlanders.
FAIRY:	I begin to understand.
FOSTER:	I served with some distinction as a soldier for nearly three days. But I became disgusted with the service on account of the brutality of the regimental barber who cut my hair so short as to render it absolutely unbecoming. (PAUSE) You don't think this was a frivolous reason for quitting the regiment?
FAIRY:	Not at all. We fairies value an elegant appearance above all things.
FOSTER:	Unfortunately the regiment took a dim view of my departure. It regarded it as desertion.
FAIRY:	So now I understand your terror of the Highland sergeant who might have recognised you. So let us consider how my fairy powers could –
FOSTER:	(CUTTING IN) I'm afraid there's more. I felt that a life of comparative seclusion would best harmonise with my then state of mind so I shipped myself away as a stowaway on The Pickled Mermaid - a ship then loading in the London

FAIRY:	Docks and due to set sail for New York forthwith. Would it help your tale if I magicked up some aural effects to render it more lifelike?
FOSTER:	That would be wonderful, fairy – er miss.

(SOUNDS OF THE ROLLING OCEAN.)

FOSTER:	After twelve days behind a pork cask, I was discovered by the boatswain who introduced me to Captain Bonecutter who received me with open arms and closed fists. The Captain's big dog, Jupiter, had just been washed overboard and Captain Bonesetter, with the unaffected hospitality of a true sailor, immediately placed the animal's kennel at my disposal.
FAIRY:	That was remarkably generous of him.
FOSTER:	From some points of view.

(SOUNDS OF FOSTER YELPING AND BARKING DOG-LIKE.)

FOSTER:	It was Captain Bonecutter's whim to treat me as if I really was a dog. And I, of course, entered into the spirit of the joke. I barked, ran about on all fours, sat up on my haunches and caught a biscuit off my

	nose. Not least because I was very hungry.
	(BACK TO ROLLING SEAS.)
FOSTER:	The joke lasted nine weeks and five days until we landed. After that I was placed ashore with a roving commission to go just wherever I pleased. So I headed for New York.
	(SOUNDS OF BUSY CITY)
FOSTER:	But I only got as far as Port Monmouth.
FAIRY:	Sorry!
	(SOUNDS OF SMALL HICK TOWN.)
FOSTER:	In Port Monmouth I made use of my mysterious arrival and English accent to create a new and altogether magnificent new personality for myself.
FAIRY:	You threw off your old bad ways and reformed?
FOSTER:	I pretended to be an English aristocrat with money to burn. They were trusting folk. They did not know how poor and destitute our English aristocracy really are. And so I came to meet the Reverend Hicks K. Plappy – my future father-in-law.

	SOUNDS OF DISTANT HYMN SINGING.)
FAIRY:	(PIOUSLY) And you confessed to him all your wrongdoings?
FOSTER:	No, I persuaded him that I wanted to build a cathedral in Port Monmouth and found a bishopric there. The Reverend Hicks K Plappy, of course, became convinced he was to be the new bishop.
	(HYMN SINGING FADES)
FAIRY:	You know – I'm not altogether sure I like this story. After all, I am very much a good fairy.
FOSTER:	Then I shall deal with the latter stages of my story briefly. In expectation of preferment the Reverend Plappy gave me his lovely daughter Louisa in marriage. I left Port Monmouth with the voices of the grateful populace ringing in my ears. They expected me to return from England with the money I had promised them for their cathedral.
FAIRY:	And this is how long ago?
FOSTER:	Seven years.
FAIRY:	Your wife has not questioned you about why you are a confectioner not an aristocrat and about why you don't have the money to build a cathedral and endow a bishopric?

FOSTER:	Louisa is a sweet trusting girl. She does not have an enquiring mind.
FAIRY:	Obviously.
FOSTER:	I've had a very good run for my money – until now. So many people could catch me out. But nobody has – until that damned Highlander sergeant –
FAIRY:	Language!
FOSTER:	Sorry, miss! Until that sergeant appeared to recognise me. I reckon it's all up with me now.
FAIRY:	On reflection, it seems to me, Mr Foster, that your career has been a very discreditable one.
FOSTER:	I'm not proud of it, miss. I've done many things in my time that I've had reason to regret. There are many incidents in my career that I'd give anything to blot out.
FAIRY:	Are you sure?
FOSTER:	Of course, I'm sure!
FAIRY:	Then I think I may be able to help you.
FOSTER:	That's very kind of you – but why?
FAIRY:	Because it's the sort of thing fairies are expected to do. Now first of all how many ornaments are there on top of that twelfth-cake in the window?
FOSTER:	Three large ones. A ship – the one you nearly tripped over. A Harlequin. And a policeman. There are also crackers and some other unimportant trifles.

FAIRY:	Forget about those. Take the three large ornaments off the cake.
FOSTER:	(TAKING THEM) Ship – harlequin – policeman. What now?
FAIRY:	Whenever you wish to obliterate any one deed of your life and all its consequences – eat one of those ornaments.
FOSTER:	You mean – every time I eat one of these cake decorations, the deed in question will be obliterated from my history?
FAIRY:	Entirely obliterated. You will be as though the deed in question had never been committed.
FOSTER:	I am very much obliged to you.
FAIRY:	Not at all. I'm very glad to have had it in my power to assist you.
	(A MAGIC PING!)
GILBERT:	(V.O.) And with that the fairy leapt daintily back on to the top of the twelfth-cake and became plaster-of-Paris once more. Cyril Foster stood in a daze.
FOSTER:	I mean, nobody believes in fairies. But there she was. But the idea I could obliterate any event in my life by eating one of these ornaments – it's frankly ridiculous.
	(THE SHOP BELL GOES AND THE DOOR OPENS.)
SERGEANT:	Excuse me, sir –

FOSTER:	No!
SERGEANT:	I wanted to ask you something –
FOSTER:	No, no, I'm not him. I'm someone else. It's all gone. It's nothing to do with me.
SERGEANT:	It's just that I was wondering –
FOSTER:	No! no!

(STRANGE OTHERWORLDLY SOUNDS)

FOSTER:	Oh no, it's too awful. I'm going to torn away from my beloved wife and adored children. He knows me for a deserter.
GILBERT:	(V.O.) Drowning men clutch at straws and Mr Foster got hold of the plaster-of-Paris ship and crunched it in his mouth.
FOSTER:	I wish – I wish – that the consequences of my desertion from the army may be obliterated from my history for ever!

(THUNDERBOLTS, LOUD COSMIC EFFECTS.)
(THEN SUDDENLY SILENCE. THEN GENTLY LAPPING WATER.)

GILBERT:	(V.O.) The confectioner's shop, the house, the street, the Scottish sergeant, the twelfth-cake, all had vanished in a moment. Mr Foster found himself lying in a comfortable cot in a ship's stern-cabin. He looked round

carefully but there wasn't a dog kennel in sight.

(CABIN DOOR BURSTS OPEN.)

JAKE: (COD PIRATICAL) Ahoy there, cap'n, it's seven bells.
FOSTER: Sorry ?
JAKE: It's seven bells.
FOSTER: Oh. (PAUSE) Cap'n, did you say?
JAKE: Aye, aye, cap'n!
FOSTER: Captain Foster?
JAKE: Aye, aye, cap'n. That be your name.
FOSTER: Er – tell the men – the crew – that I'll come upstairs – er be on deck in three whisks of a monkey's tail.
JAKE: Aye, aye, cap'n.
FOSTER: And aye, aye to you.

(THE CABIN DOOR CLOSES AGAIN.)

GILBERT: (V.O.) Mr Foster had determined to be surprised by nothing. He would leave it to time and accident to enlighten him as to the circumstances in which he found himself. Accordingly he dressed himself in a pair of blue serge trousers –
FOSTER: Ah, good.
GILBERT: (V.O.) - in the pockets of which were the Policeman and the Harlequin —a pea-jacket with a

	gilt button – and a cap with a gold band.
	(FOSTER HUMS: "Oh I am the Captain of the Pinafore" FROM H.M.S. PINAFORE.)
GILBERT:	(V.O.) Remember please – no Sullivan. (SILENCE) Thank you. Fully dressed, Captain Foster went on deck.
	(CROSSFADE TO DISCREETLY ROLLING SEAS AND BRACING SEA BREEZE.)
SAMUEL:	(ANOTHER COD PIRATE) Morning, cap'n.
FOSTER:	Good morning.
SAMUEL:	You know, cap'n, with a breeze like this I reckon we shall take tarnations snakes out of yon scurvy British frigate.
FOSTER:	Indeed. Now where precisely is the yon British frigate to which you so graphically refer?
SAMUEL:	About three miles off the starboard quarter, cap'n. Grab 'ee hold of my telescope.
FOSTER:	(AS IF LOOKING THROUGH TELESCOPE) Ah yes, I see can him – I mean her.
SAMUEL:	If this breeze lasts she'll never overhaul The Flying Clam.
FOSTER:	Indeed. But if she should overhaul us – The Flying Clam that is - who cares?
SAMUEL:	(STARTLED) Well, I do, cap'n.

JAKE:	And I do, cap'n.
SAMUEL:	And so do the rest of the crew.
FOSTER:	(CAUTIOUSLY) Any particular reason?
SAMUEL:	Any partickler reason? Oh, cap'n, you always were a wag, Weren't he, Jake?
JAKE:	Oh, yes, Cap'n Foster's a wag all right!

(THEY BOTH LAUGH HEARTILY. THE SEA BREEZE CONTINUES.)

GILBERT:	(V.O.) Mr Foster joined in with his crew's merriment but had an uncomfortable feeling that he was missing out on the essential joke that so amused them. He looked vainly around the deck for enlightenment. Then a sailor scrambled up one of the masts and he happened to look up. What he saw proudly blowing in the wind took his breath away.

(A SUDDEN STRANGLED CRY FROM FOSTER.)

FOSTER:	(QUIETLY) Oh, my goodness.
SAMUEL:	Anything the matter, cap'n?
FOSTER:	I – I was just admiring our flag. Do you think we ought to maybe take it down? I mean, a skull and crossbones it is a bit well, how shall I put it? Ostentatious. It's rather like advertising we're pirates, isn't it?
JAKE:	But we are pirates, cap'n.

SAMUEL:	Always have been pirates.
JAKE:	Always will be.
FOSTER:	But all the same –
JAKE:	You wouldn't have us betray the flag now would 'ee, cap'n?
FOSTER:	No, but –
SAMUEL:	Ain't no point anyway. 'Tis known the high seas over that The Flying Clam be a pirate ship. Ain't it, Jake?
JAKE:	That it be, Samuel.
FOSTER:	We could have changed the name of the ship. Couldn't we?
SAMUEL:	We tried, cap'n. We called it H.M.S. Pinafore but the name never caught on.
FOSTER:	(DEEP GULP) So here we are then. I am the Captain of a pirate ship –
SAMUEL:	A ship laden with stolen booty.
JAKE:	That's why we're not moving so fast.
FOSTER:	(DEEPER GULP) So I am the Captain of a very slow-moving pirate ship currently being hotly pursued by one of Her Britannic Majesty's ships of war. And – let me get this clear – they are moving faster than we are.
JAKE:	That's it, cap'n. You always did have a lovely way with words.
SAMUEL:	That's why we've kept you on as cap'n. Even though you're one of the worst navigators the top and bottom of the Seven Seas.
FOSTER:	Still – you did mention the favourable breeze that will

JAKE:	enable us to escape the Britisher? Aye, aye, cap'n, while that breeze favours us they'll never catch us.

(THE BREEZE SUDDENLY STOPS BLOWING.)

SAMUEL:	Oh, dear, that's unfortunate, cap'n.
FOSTER:	What is?
JAKE:	The breeze has stopped blowing.

(A DIFFERENT SOUND OF WIND)

SAMUEL:	Reckon the wind's shifted in their favour, cap'n.
JAKE:	Should be grappling with us in no time at all.
FOSTER:	Well, maybe something'll turn up, eh?

(HE WHISTLES Rule Britannia QUIETLY.)

GILBERT:	(V.O.) Mr Foster was beginning to realise the full meaning of the phrase – out of the frying pan and into the fire. It was becoming clear to him that if he had not deserted from the army when he did, he would have ended up commanding a pirate ship. It did not seem to him a very plausible turn of events but at that moment he was not in any position to question its

likelihood – for the British frigate was pressing towards them.

(DISTANT CANNON FIRE. SOUNDS OF THE CREW ASSEMBLING ON DECK.)

JAKE: Crew awaiting your orders, cap'n.

FOSTER: Well, er – Jake – perhaps you'd like to fill them in on what we have planned.

JAKE: Aye, aye, cap'n. (RAISING HIS VOICE) Right, my shipmates, listen here to me. See this 'ere slow match.

(THE CREW SAYS: Aye, aye…)

JAKE: And you see it's attached to the end of this 'ere piece of yarn which lies across the deck 'ere.

(THE CREW SAYS: Aye, aye…)

JAKE: Well, this 'ere piece of yarn is attached to an open barrel of gunpowder in the magazine, just as the cap'n ordered.

SAMUEL: So you see what'll happen, shipmates?

(THE CREW SAYS: Aye, aye…)

SAMUEL: We fight on but as soon as the Britisher's first shot strikes our hull, we're done for. So I lights this slow match. It's in beautiful order and burns two minutes. And then –

JAKE: Boom!!! Up we goes, and there's an end to The Flying Clam, crew, cargo, cap'n and all.

(ROARS OF APPROVAL FROM CREW.)

FOSTER: Just a moment – I've been thinking. If we blow ourselves up they may say that we do so because we are afraid of them! The thought is endurable! No, no – let us rather express our indifference to penal servitude by submitting with sullen contempt to whatever punishment these bloodhounds may think proper to inflict upon us.

(MURMURINGS FROM THE CREW.)

SAMUEL: I don't believe my ears. Is this our cap'n speaking, Jake?

JAKE: He's showing the white feather, Samuel. This 'ere cap'n of ours – this white-livered devil's chicken – he's a slinkin' coward, a shiverin' cocktail!

SAMUEL:	He won't fight and he won't sink – he's going to give in, shipmates – if you let him!

(THE MUTINOUS NOISES GET LOUDER.)

FOSTER:	No, no, you misunderstand me. I –
JAKE:	So what is your programme, cap'n?
SAMUEL:	What do you purpose to do?
FOSTER:	Why, to fight till the last drop of my blood shall trickle on these snowy decks and then – light the slow match!

(CHEERS FROM CREW.)

JAKE:	Brave cap'n.
SAMUEL:	Well said!
GILBERT:	(V.O.) Meanwhile the British frigate – to which nobody had been paying very attention during all this excitement – came closer and closer.

(THE BOOM OF A CANNON FOLLOWED BY ITS LANDING AND A HUGE EXPLOSION.)

GILBERT:	(V.O.) With their first shot, the crew of the British frigate blew a big hole in the hull of <u>The Flying Clam</u>. Further resistance was useless. Mr Foster knew at once what he must do.

FOSTER:	(DRAMATICALLY) Samuel – light the slow match!
SAMUEL:	Aye, aye, cap'n.
	(SOUND OF A SIZZLING FUSE)
GILBERT:	(V.O.) Mr Foster took out his watch –
FOSTER:	(CALMLY) In two minutes we shall all be blown to smithereens.
JAKE:	Abandon ship!
SAMUEL:	Abandon ship!
	(SOUNDS OF PANIC AND PEOPLE JUMPING OVERBOARD.)
GILBERT:	(V.O.) The pirates flung themselves overboard in an orgy of panic. But Mr Foster stayed calm. He looked at his watch for a minute and a half. Then he reached into his pocket and took out the plaster-of-Paris policeman. He started to crunch it.
FOSTER:	(MOUTH FULL) I now wish that all the consequences of my ever going to sea may be blotted out of my history for ever!
	(THUNDERBOLTS, LOUD COSMIC EFFECTS.) (THEN THE STATELY TICKING OF A CLOCK.)

GILBERT:	(V.O.) Mr Foster found himself seated at a handsome mahogany writing-table. Beneath his feet was an Axminster carpet of astonishing pile – and above a handsome marble mantelpiece hung a portrait of himself in the act of making a speech.
FOSTER:	Now this is more like it!
GILBERT:	(V.O.) But where was he? The room was fitted up partly as an office, partly as a study. He picked up a sheet of writing paper from a stand on the desk.
FOSTER:	(RUSTLE OF PAPER AS HE READS) Royal Indelible Bank, 142 Threadneedle Street, E.C. (PAUSE) Mmm, I must be some sort of banker's clerk. In a pretty impressive looking concern too. Now let's see –
	(A DOOR IS OPENED.)
GILBERT:	(V.O.) Mr Foster opened the door and found it communicated with a very large room in which forty or fifty clerks were at work in far humbler conditions than his own.
FOSTER:	Banker's clerk be hanged! I'm a banker, or something like it, and on a large scale too!
	(THE CLOCK STARTS TO STRIKE FIVE.)
GILBERT:	(V.O.) The clock struck five. All the clerks rose simultaneously

	and started to go home, bowing respectfully to Mr Foster as they went.
FOSTER:	I suppose I ought to go to. I wonder where I live?
GILBERT:	(V.O.) He took down his hat from the peg and followed the last clerk out. At the end of a passage a porter was respectfully holding the door open for him. Mr Foster was about to ask him where he lived but felt this might sound a little foolish. But anyway before he could speak –
PORTER:	Your carriage is here, sir.
	(A SOUND OF A CARRIAGE APPROACHING.)
GILBERT:	(V.O.) A brougham drawn by a pair of handsome greys pulled up at the door. Relieved, Mr Foster got in.
FOSTER:	Home! And don't spare the horses.
	(THE RATTLE OF A HORSE-DRAWN CARRIAGE OVER CITY STREETS.)
GILBERT:	(V.O.) Mr Foster leant back on the soft cushions and wondered where he was heading.
FOSTER:	Now this is something like it. I've got a good berth – secretary or manager perhaps – in a substantial Bank – and no doubt

	I'm being driven to some snug little villa in Regent's Park – or maybe a house in Bedford Square - with Louise and the children waiting for me.
	(THE CARRIAGE RATTLES ON.)
GILBERT:	(V.O.) But the carriage didn't stop in Regent's Park or Bedford Square. It drove down Oxford Street and past Marble Arch towards Bayswater.
FOSTER:	I'm not going to live in Bayswater! If it's Bayswater then I'll move tomorrow.
GILBERT:	(V.O.) But to his amazement the carriage drove into Lancaster Gate – and stopped at No.352. In a daze, Mr Foster descended. The door was opened by an imposing figure in livery.
	(A BIG FRONT DOOR CREAKS OPEN.)
SERVANT:	Good evening, Sir Cyril.
FOSTER:	(QUIETLY) Sir Cyril, eh? Sir Cyril Foster! Sounds good. (ALOUD:) Is anybody in?
SERVANT:	Only my lady, Sir Cyril.
FOSTER:	Only your lady?
SERVANT:	Yes, Sir Cyril. Her ladyship is upstairs.
FOSTER:	Is she now?
	(THE DOOR IS SHUT. FEET RUNNING UPSTAIRS.)

GILBERT:	(V.O.) Mr Foster ran upstairs without stopping to examine his magnificent surroundings. To be reunited with his Louisa in these circumstances was a joy beyond measure. He rushed into the drawing room.
	(OPENING OF INNER DOOR. PATTER OF TINY FEET.)
TODDLER:	(OF EITHER SEX AS AVAILABLE) Papa, papa!
GILBERT:	(V.O.) A small child tottered towards him smiling broadly. Mr Foster did not recognise it as one of his.
TODDLER:	Papa's comes home!
FOSTER:	I'm very sorry, little one but I'm not your papa.
	(SCREAMS AND HYSTERICS FROM THE CHILD.)
LADY FOSTER:	(APPROACHING) Cyril – what are you doing? On this day of all days!
GILBERT:	(V.O.) The lady who approached was buxom and pleasant-looking but assuredly she was not Mr Foster's wife.
LADY FOSTER:	My dear, welcome home.
	(A KISS)
LADY FOSTER:	But what on earth do you mean by upsetting our dear little child on a day like this?

FOSTER:	It – it was a joke. Of course, I know that's my child. Just as I know that you're my wife. You must be my wife after all mustn't you? Otherwise I wouldn't be here and you wouldn't be there and –
LADY FOSTER:	(CUTTING IN) Cyril, is there something wrong in the City?
FOSTER:	No, no. Nothing whatever – dear.
LADY FOSTER:	No secrets from little wifey now?
FOSTER:	Everything's quite wonderful.
LADY FOSTER:	Then go and get ready for dinner. On this our very special day.
	(ANOTHER DECOROUS KISS.)
GILBERT:	(V.O.) Mr Foster – now known as Sir Cyril – retired to his dressing-room to prepare for dinner. Fortunatelt a valet ushered him in so he didn't have to ask the way. As he dressed - with the plaster-of-Paris Harlequin safe in his pocket - he considered his situation.
FOSTER:	(GETTING CHANGED) Well, I suppose as a speculation this change hasn't turned out too badly. I have exchanged a lawless life of continual peril for one of assured prosperity and perfect lawfulness. Of course, I shall miss Louisa since my new

	wife cannot hold a candle to her. But such, I suppose, is life.
	(FEET DOWN STEPS)
GILBERT:	(V.O.) A little later Mr – Sir – Cyril Foster descended the stairs dressed for dinner. Fortunately the same servant was still in the hall.
FOSTER:	(CONFIDENTLY) So who has arrived for supper?
SERVANT:	Mr and Mrs Bortle and Lord Portico, Sir Cyril.
FOSTER:	Very good. Remind me – nobody else is invited tonight, are they?
SERVANT:	No, nobody at all, Sir Cyril. It's a <u>souper intime</u>.
FOSTER:	I just wanted to be certain. The fatigues of the City you understand. (DEEP BREATH) Well, I wonder what they are all going to be like.
	(DOOR PULLED OPEN. POLITE BUZZ OF CONVERSATION.)
PORTICO:	(ELDERLY ARISTOCRAT) Ah, Sir Cyril!
FOSTER:	(GUESSING) My dear Lord Portico.
PORTICO:	Congratulations on this happy event!
FOSTER:	Thank you. I'm so sorry that dear Lady Portico could not join us.

(A FROSTY PAUSE.)

PORTICO: It would be difficult to bring her here from the Portico Family Mauseoleum.
FOSTER: She – she's not well?
PORTICO: She's been dead for six months.
FOSTER: Ah!
BORTLE: (APPROACHING) Foster – how are you doing?
FOSTER: I'm very well. And you? Mr Bortle? Have I got that right?
BORTLE: (STIFFLY) I should hope you have.
FOSTER: I – I should know the name?
BORTLE: (PO-FACED) Very funny, Cyril. I've always enjoyed your sense of humour. So has your wife.
FOSTER: My wife?
BORTLE: My daughter.
FOSTER: Ah!

(THE BUZZ OF DINNER PARTY CONVERSATION.)

GILBERT: (V.O.) Mr Foster managed to bluff his way through dinner adequately enough. But no amount of enquiry enabled him to find out what happy event this dinner was supposed to be celebrating. Frankly, even the name of his wife would have been a useful clue.

(THE BUZZ OF CONVERSATION QUIETENS.)

GILBERT: (V.O.) After dinner Lord Portico rose to his feet.

PORTICO: Ladies and gentlemen, it is not usual to drink healths at modern dinner parties but there are occasions when the strict forms of etiquette must be relaxed. I do not need to detain you by dilating on the auspicious character of the event we are here to celebrate. I will content myself with proposing the health of Sir Cyril ands his admirable wife.

(A MURMUR OF APPROVAL FROM THE GUESTS.)

GILBERT: (V.O.) From Mr Foster's point of view, there could not have been a less illuminating toast. He still didn't know what the dinner was celebrating. He didn't know his child's name. He didn't know his wife's name. Here, if ever, he had to rely upon his own resourcefulness. His instinct was that this was the anniversary of his wedding.

(THE BUZZ OF THE DINNER PARTY.)

FOSTER: (RISING) Ladies and gentlemen, my dear, my very, very dear old friend –

GILBERT: (V.O.) He'd forgotten his name.

FOSTER:	In replying on behalf of my dear wife and myself –
GILBERT:	(V.O.) Mr Foster still had to work out what the purpose of this celebration was. He took a leap into the dark.
FOSTER:	On this day - never mind how many years ago – Heaven blessed our union.
	(THE ASSEMBLED GUESTS GO: Ah Yes!!)
BORTLE:	Only four years ago, dear boy.
FOSTER:	Ah yes, of course. Four years ago. So – on this day four years ago, my wife and I were married.
	(A SHRIEK FROM LADY FOSTER.)
LADY FOSTER:	Cyril – what are you saying?
FOSTER:	I am saying – my love – that on this days four years ago, on this day of all others, you and I were married –
	(ANOTHER EVEN SHRILLER SHRIEK – FOLLOWED BY A THUD.)
GILBERT:	(V.O.) Lady Foster screamed and fainted. Her father was outraged.
BORTLE:	Cyril, you're drunk – drunk at your own table!
PORTICO:	I say, please be composed, Mr Bortle.

BORTLE:	I will not be composed, Lord Portico. We have been invited here to celebrate the fourth anniversary of the birth of my daughter's son and heir. And this insolent joker, whose fortune I and my daughter have made – rises and states - at his own table – that on this day four years ago, and on this day of all others, and not until this day, he and she were happily married. (A GROAN) Happily married!
	(A UNIVERSAL GROAN.)
GILBERT:	(V.O.) Despite the uproar, Mr Foster was enormously relieved to discover the significance of the dinner he was attending. It would have been helpful to learn the name of his wife but you cannot expect everything. He was about to respond to Mr Bortle when a servant entered with a note -
SERVANT:	(SOTTO VOCE) I'm sorry, Sir Cyril, but they insisted.
	(A RUSTLE OF PAPER.)
GILBERT:	(V.O.) Mr Foster was all too happy to take the opportunity to leave the dinner party and talk to the gentlemen in question.
	(HALL ACCOUSTIC:)
POLICEMAN:	Sir Cyril Foster?

FOSTER:	Yes?
POLICEMAN:	I think you know why we're here.
FOSTER:	Well, actually, the note was a little vague but –
POLICEMAN:	But I presume you'll still be happy to accompany us?
FOSTER:	Of course. Where are we going?
POLICEMAN;	(DRY LAUGH) Oh, Sir Cyril, we'd heard about your sense of humour.
FOSTER:	So I'm going to be away for some time?
POLICEMAN:	Depends what the jury make of a case of persistent financial fraud.
FOSTER:	What?
POLICEMAN:	Sir Cyril, what would would say is my line of business is that you've had a good run for your money.
FOSTER:	You're saying I'm a financial fraud?
POLICEMAN:	Of course not, sir. That's not my job. It's down to the jury.
	(THE BABBLE OF A COURT ROOM.)
GILBERT:	(V.O.) Mr Foster had no substantial defence not least because he had no idea what the charges meant. But he threw himself upon the Court in a speech which has been preserved in the annals of the Old Bailey as the type of what such speeches should be.

(THE HUM OF THE COURT ROOM UNDER:)

FOSTER: My lord, and gentlemen of the jury, I cannot deny that I – before I was me – may have been guilty of the crime imputed to me by the learned counsel for the prosecution. But reflect. I have been for some hours past the toy and sport of a Twelfth Cake fairy, who has encouraged me to alter the circumstances of my life in a most irresponsible way. That fairy, gentlemen, has been the curse of my life. Let it be a warning to you all to beware of supernatural assistance. Trust to your own exertions and you'll all do very well. I know that you are about to return a verdict of guilty –

(A MURMUR OF ASSENT)

FOSTER: Followed by a sentence of penal servitude for life –

(ANOTHER MURMUR OF ASSENT.)

FOSTER: All I can say by way of response is that the best thing I can do is to make another change in my condition with all possible response.

GILBERT:	(V.O.) Here, it is recorded in the annals of the Old Bailey, the defendant removed a plaster-of-Paris cake decoration representing a Harlequin from his pocket and started to chew it.
	(THUNDERBOLTS, LOUD COSMIC EFFECTS.) (THEN RETURN TO THE SHOP ACCOUSTIC.)
GILBERT:	(V.O.) And behold! Mr Cyril Foster found himself once more in his little confectionary shop in the Borough Road. He was in the act of selling the Twelfth Cake with the Policeman, the Ship and the Harlequin on top to a female customer.
FOSTER:	I'm very sorry, madam, but the fairy on the top seems to have disappeared.
CUSTOMER:	(SHE HAS THE FAIRY'S VOICE) I quite understand, Mr Foster. Whenever you need a fairy, you can never find one.
	(THE MYSTERIOUS PING!)
GILBERT:	(V.O.) To Mr Foster's relief, Louisa was still in the back shop with the children. He related to her the history of his adventure. She refused to believe him and told him he was a silly boy who had been dreaming. Which, now I come to think of it, is very probably the case.

(FADE TO CLOSING MUSIC AND CREDITS.)

THE END

A SENSATION NOVEL

First broadcast on Radio 4 on 22nd December 2004 with the following cast –

GILBERT	Jonathan Coy
EBENEZER FUDGE	John Rowe
DEMON / GRIPPER	Nick Boulton
LADY ROCKALDA	Julia Hills
SIR RUTHVEN	Hugh Dickson
HERBERT	Jason Chan
ALICE GREY	Wendy Baxter

The director was JENNY STEPHENS

	(GILBERT'S VOICE IS HEARD SPEAKING SLOWLY AS IF WORKING THIS OUT FOR THE FIRST TIME.)
GILBERT:	(V.O.) I am very good at integral and differential calculus... (PAUSE) I know the scientific names of ... of beings animalculous... (SLOWLY) Animalculous? Calculus? Balculus? Dalculus?
	(A SUDDEN BURST OF THE OVERTURE TO THE PIRATES OF PENZANCE. IT'S CUT OFF)
GILBERT:	(V.O.) That's quite enough, thank you. (CLEARS THROAT) Today's story from the pen of W.S.Gilbert uncontrolled by the baton of Sir Arthur Sullivan is called A Sensation Novel – and it is, I will admit, rather a strange tale.
	(CUT TO PEN ON PAPER.)
FUDGE:	(WRITING) "Unhand me, sir!" she cried indignantly as she" – oh, no, no.
	(A WEARY SIGH FOLLOWED BY COUGHING.)
GILBERT:	(V.O.) Mr Ebenezer Fudge had been one of the nineteenth

century's most prolific and successful authors. Novels dropped from his pen at the rate of three to four a year, all in three-volume form. They were mostly 'sensation' novels filled with dark deeds and exciting events. Who could ever forget "The Woman in Puce" – or "Lady Awful's Secret" – or "She Knew it was Wrong – but she did it anyway"? But the sad fact was that such a prodigious rate of production comes at a price – and Mr Ebenezer Fudge was starting to pay it…

FUDGE: (WRITING) " 'Unclasp those unprincipled digits from my person', she exclaimed, 'or I'll…' " (ANOTHER SIGH) Oh no, no, no….

(ANOTHER SIGH. THEN THE CLINK OF GLASS AND BOTTLE FOLLOWED BY A LONG DRINK.)

GILBERT: (V.O.) The sad fact was that in search of inspiration Mr Ebenezer Fudge had taken to the bottle. And an even sadder fact was that the bottle was increasingly giving him back very little in return. He was at work on a new three-volume sensation novel – as yet untitled – which was due at his publishers in three weeks. But

	nothing was working, however long the midnight gin was quaffed.
FUDGE:	(WRITING) "Remove that part of your body which extends from your wrist to your fingernails from its current location, " she bellowed, "or I'll....."
	(ANOTHER SIGH, ANOTHER DRINK)
GILBERT:	(V.O.) Maybe it was the strain, maybe the excess of alcohol but as he was working something very odd indeed happened.
	(THE 'RUDDIGORE' GHOST MUSIC.)
FUDGE:	(GASPING) Ahhhhh…
GILBERT:	(V.O.) There seated on the other side of the desk – even though there wasn't a seat – was a pale, lurid figure with bright red eyes.
FUDGE:	Who – who are you?
DEMON:	I am the Demon of Romance.
FUDGE:	I beg your pardon?
DEMON:	The Demon of Romance!!! Remember our deadly pact?
FUDGE:	Nnnnn – no!
DEMON:	It is thanks to me that you are able to produce so many three-volume sensation novels at such a prodigious rate.
FUDGE:	Then help me – please.

DEMON:	First let us be clear – in this current work of fiction, have you been employing all the characters I supplied? The virtuous governess, the unemployed young Sunday school teacher, the sensation detective, the wicked baronet – and the beautiful villainess with the yellow hair and the panther-like movement?
FUDGE:	I have.
DEMON:	You have made the virtuous governess in love with the Sunday school teacher? You have made her persecuted by the wicked baronet?
FUDGE:	Of course.
DEMON:	The yellow-haired harpy with the panther-like movement is his accomplice?
FUDGE:	She is!
DEMON:	Have you made <u>her</u> fall in love with the Sunday school teacher?
FUDGE:	Head and ears.
DEMON:	And he treats her with disdain?
FUDGE:	He does!
DEMON:	Humph! You have put live shrimps down your back to make your flesh creep?
FUDGE:	Pints of them.
DEMON:	You've read the "Illustrated Police News"?
FUDGE:	From cover to cover.
DEMON:	Then why aren't things working?
FUDGE:	That's what I want to know. You're the supernatural figure around here, you tell me.

DEMON:	You are in my power!
FUDGE:	So you've said.
DEMON:	But then so are your characters. These creatures I have lent you are slaves to my will. They are accepted types and you can't get on without them.
FUDGE:	Yes, but what is the nature of the power you exercise over them?
DEMON:	It is very peculiar.
FUDGE:	I've no doubt of that.
DEMON:	They are all creatures who in their mortal condition, have been guilty of positive or negative crime, and they are compelled to personate, under my direction, those stock characters of the sensation novelist which are most opposed to their individual tastes and inclinations.
FUDGE:	So you're saying that they have an existence apart from that with which they are endowed in the novel?
DEMON:	They have!
FUDGE:	This is absurd! Incredible! You're asking me to believe –
DEMON:	(FIRMLY) I don't think anybody who wrote the climax of your last novel has any right to call anything absurd or incredible. They have a separate existence, yes, that is to say, they have wishes, schemes and plans of their own, but the fulfilment of these wishes is, for the time being, in the hands of

	the author to whom they are entrusted.
FUDGE:	This is getting absurder by the moment! I've not even started the second bottle of gin yet!

(MORE GHOSTLY MUSIC. THEN CREAKY FLOORBOARDS, GHOSTLY EFFECTS)

FUDGE:	Aaargh!!
ROCKALDA:	(SOFTLY) In this dark room, she thought, many dark deeds have been committed, the floor is full of traps which open with springs – suddenly!
FUDGE:	It – it can't be!
GILBERT:	(V.O.) But it was. There just beyond his desk was his lovely villainess, the Lady Rockalda, a candle in her hand, making her way across the ruined summer house, overlooking the Thames, he had just described in chapter eleven of volume one.
FUDGE:	But – how come she's here?
DEMON:	These creatures have the power of coming to life at the end of the first – and second – volumes, and immediately before the last chapter of the third, to talk over the events that have taken place and to arrange plans for the future. Plans which are too often frustrated by the Author's arbitrary will. This is not generally known.

FUDGE: I'll say it isn't! I swear I'll never touch gin again.

DEMON: Too late. Your characters are assembling because you have just completed the first volume –

FUDGE: But it's terrible, the worst thing I've ever done –

DEMON: Don't you think they know how bad it is?

ROCKALDA: (TO HERSELF) Would he never come? But even her indomitable nerve snapped when a door opened suddenly behind her. (BLAND VOICE) End of Volume One.

DEMON: (SOFTLY) I'll leave you now –

FUDGE: But –

DEMON: The others will be here – very soon.

(A WHOOSH AS THE DEMON DISAPPEARS)

GILBERT: (V.O.) Now normally when a ghost disappears with a whoosh like that, it means the nightmare is over. But Ebenezer Fudge realised he was still locked in a room with one of his own characters.

(MORE CREAKING FLOORBOARDS, HORROR FX)

GILBERT: (V.O.) And then before he knew it – Sir Ruthven Glenaloon, his wicked baronet, also carrying a

	candle had joined Lady Rockalda.
RUTHVEN:	(SOFTLY) Rockalda, are you there?
ROCKALDA:	Yes – the first volume is over. We are free for a little while.
RUTHVEN:	It is so very hard to be a wicked baronet against one's will. When I was I was the softest hearted fellow alive – when I was alive.
ROCKALDA:	But you still did a great deal of damage by generously giving indiscriminate donations to ridiculously-named charities which turned out to be fraudulent or worse.
RUTHVEN:	That is true. And you had five strapping sons and being an indulgent mother, you let them all have their own way with unsavoury and unpredictable consequences. They broke several windows, I believe.
	(MORE CREAKING FLOORBOARDS, HORROR FX)
ROCKALDA:	You know I really don't like this summerhouse overlooking the Thames.
RUTHVEN:	Nor do I. I'm by temperament a timid and nervous man and I don't feel at all comfortable here.

ROCKALDA: And yet we are supposed to revel in its gloom and –

ROCKALDA: (WITH A SIGH) Hush! Here comes the good young man of the novel!

(MORE FEET OVER CREAKY FLOOR BOARDS)

FUDGE: Him as well!

GILBERT: (V.O.) For through the gloom came Herbert, the virtuous Sunday School teacher.

FUDGE: He's not supposed to come here until Volume 2 when they set a trap for him and submerge him in the Teddington lock.

GILBERT: (V.O.) But here he was!

HERBERT: (APPROACHING THE OTHERS) Rockalda! At last we meet!

(A KISS)

FUDGE: He can't do that! She's a wicked wanton!

GILBERT: (V.O.) But he did!
HERBERT: Dear Rockalda, how delightful to see you. Let me see, wasn't the last time we met was at the end of the Indian novel? "Seize her – she is not my aunt after all!" I think was the line.

ROCKALDA: Indeed. (WITH A SIGH) You were a mild young artist travelling in India.

204

HERBERT:	And you were the yellow-haired Begum of the Rajah of Babbetyboobledore.
RUTHVEN:	And I was the Rajah's villainous Grand Vizier. Accurate historical research never being our author's strong point.
HERBERT:	Well, you're being a real villain in this one, Ruthven.
RUTHVEN:	I'll say! We've only got to the end of the first volume and I've already committed a burglary, a forgery, a falsification of a baptismal entry. And I'll lay twenty to one I try to murder you, Herbert, before I'm done.
HERBERT:	And I'll take you twenty to one you don't succeed.
RUTHVEN:	Of course not. You're the good young man and – you've got to marry Alice.
HERBERT:	Please – don't remind me.
RUTHVEN:	Who is really <u>my</u> Alice, whom I love devotedly – and who loves me.
HERBERT:	Yes, <u>out</u> of the novel.
RUTHVEN:	Exactly! In the novel, she detests me. Luckily we have an opportunity at the end of each volume to appear for an hour or so in our own true light. In my true light Alice worships me.
HERBERT:	Well, we've deserved it all.
ROCKALDA:	We have, oh, we have! What exactly did you do on earth?
HERBERT:	(BASHFULLY) I – I frequented music halls and sang comic songs of a somewhat lewd nature. As a punishment I have

	to represent the author's good young man during the term of his natural life. Horrible, isn't it?
ROCKALDA:	Vile! Because, of course, you and I can never, ever be one, however tempted you may be by my fair locks. However long I beguile you with my feminine charms, you are forced to reject me.
HERBERT:	So what a relief after making love for a whole volume to that ridiculously insipid creature, Alice Grey, to be able for a few moments to spend some time with a woman as interesting and passionate as you.
ROCKALDA:	(EMBRACING) Herbert!
HERBERT:	Rockalda!
	(MORE FEET ACROSS CREAKY FLOORBOARDS)
GILBERT:	(V.O.) And then – there was Alice Grey, the demure, modest-looking governess, a figure of whom Miss Bronte would have been proud.
ALICE:	What's this? My devoted Herbert in the arms of the detestable Lady Rockalda!
	(UNIVERSAL GROANS FROM THE OTHERS)
HERBERT:	Alice – please! I've spent the whole first volume mooning around after you. I've even had

	to write poetry to you. At least, let me enjoy myself in the few moments of relaxation permitted between volumes.
ALICE:	Of course! Let us make the most of these happy intervals for I'm sure you will marry me at the end of the third volume.
HERBERT:	(GROANING) No, there's not much doubt of that.
RUTHVEN:	But, Alice – my darling – perhaps you may not marry him after all. He may prove unworthy of you.
HERBERT:	Not much chance of that! I'm dreadfully good.
ALICE:	Exactly! Oh, Ruthven, my love –
RUTHVEN:	Yes, my dearest?
ALICE:	When our author, Mr Fudge, sets you on to persecute me with your attentions, he little dreams how ardently I hope that your nefarious schemes to make me a fallen woman might succeed. But, no, that irritating Sunday School teacher must always interfere.
HERBERT:	Not because I want to!
ALICE:	And you're such a bore in the novel too!
HERBERT:	Now, excuse me, I do think that's going a bit too far. I was rather bold with you in the scene in the pine forest in chapter eight, wasn't I?

	(GROANS OF DISBELIEF FROM FUDGE)
GILBERT:	(V.O.) By now as his own characters started to re-enact scenes from his novel with their own running commentary, Mr Fudge started to believe he was going mad. He certainly vowed never to touch another bottle of gin again.
	(ROMANTIC MUSIC. FOREST MURMURS.)
ALICE:	Chapter Eight – the Pine forest.
HERBERT:	"Miss Alice" said Herbert –
ALICE:	Miss Alice indeed! (MUSIC STOPS) I rest my case!
HERBERT:	But –
ALICE:	I'm sorry. In a pine forest – there's moonlight – and you call me <u>Miss</u> Alice! You're hopeless!
HERBERT:	Maybe but I did warm up afterwards.
	(ROMANTIC MUSIC. FOREST MURMURS.)
HERBERT:	"Miss Alice, I fear your stony-hearted guardian –"
RUTHVEN:	That's me!
HERBERT:	Do be quiet, Ruthven. (CLEARS THROAT) "I fear

	your stony-hearted guardian will never relent."
ALICE:	"You are very formal, Herbert, replied Alice."
HERBERT:	"Miss Grey – dear Alice, dearest Alice – I may call you dearest Alice, may I not?" <u>(MUSIC CUTS)</u> That was pretty warm, wasn't it?
ALICE:	Not after the demure encouragement I had given you. Still – go on.

<u>(ROMANTIC MUSIC. FOREST MURMURS.)</u>

HERBERT:	"I may call you dearest Alice, may I not?"
ALICE:	"I cannot help what you choose to call me, said the pretty girl." <u>(ASIDE)</u> Yuk!
HERBERT:	"They were alone – with the moon. They heard the throbbings of each other's hearts, which beat like rival watches, wound up in each other! He drew her gently towards him, and imprinted a solitary kiss on her soft little hand."
ALICE:	It's intolerable!

<u>(THE MUSIC CUTS)</u>

ALICE:	I mean, it's not as if you're actually going to do anything. No sooner have I responded than you flee, terrified of your own boldness. When I think of what happened in the scene after with Sir Ruthven. Now that was something.
	(HEIGHTENED DRAMATIC MUSIC)
RUTHVEN:	"Alice, said the Baronet, his cold, evil eyes lighting with a horrible fire. At last you are in my power! I heard you were in the forest and I determined to find you."
ALICE:	"Alice covered her eyes with her hands. She tried to scream, but terror had rendered her speechless…"
	(SHE BREAKS OFF. MUSIC DIES.)
ALICE:	Don't you see? It's wonderful. I could go through that scene again and again.
RUTHVEN:	I'm very happy to oblige.

(HEIGHTENED DRAMATIC MUSIC AGAIN)

RUTHVEN: "Pretty one, ignore that puling Sunday School teacher. I love you – and in love, as in war, all things are fair!"

ALICE: (SOFTLY) "Unhand me, monster!"

RUTHVEN: "Not so, pretty one. A coach and horses is in readiness in the thickest part of the forest, and I have minions who will drive you where I will. Salisbury Plain is barely fifty leagues away, a clergyman in full canonicals and an aged pew-opener are awaiting us at Stonehenge and he will speak the words that will make you mine."

ALICE: "Unhand me, sir!" she cried indignantly" (SOFTLY) Just carry on. (ALOUD) "Unclasp those unprincipled digits from my person," she exclaimed." (SOFTLY) Ignore all this. (ALOUD) "Remove that part of your body which extends from your wrist to your fingernails from its current location, " she bellowed, "or I'll….."

(SUDDENLY HERBERT STEPS IN.)

HERBERT: "Monster, unhand that lady!"

(THE MUSIC GRINDS TO A HALT.)

ALICE: You had to spoil it, didn't you?
HERBERT: It's the author's fault not mine!
RUTHVEN: You hit me!
HERBERT: I didn't mean anything by it!
RUTHVEN: But it was such a delicious scene.
ALICE: You know, Herbert, if you hadn't interrupted, we would have been comfortably married at Stonehenge and everything would have ended happily.
HERBERT: I can only agree.
ROCKALDA: So can I! Herbert and I might have been happy as well. You remember chapter seven in which I first fell in love with you?
HERBERT: Perfectly! It was at the old lime-kiln.

(CROSSFADE TO WIND THROUGH TREES)

RUTHVEN: I remember saying to you in the old mysterious forest – (INTO CHARACTER) "Rockalda, engage him in conversation at the brink of the lime kiln. I will come upon him from behind, and having stunned him with one unerring blow, I will consume his body in lime, and not so much as a button shall be left to tell the tale."

ROCKALDA: "No, Sir Ruthven, I said, if there is murder to be done, I will do it alone." So I lured you to the lime kiln under a promise that when I got you there I would reveal the secret of Alice Grey's birth."

(CROSSFADE TO BUBBLING VAT EFFECTS)

HERBERT: "Madam, I am here at your request. You have a secret that concerns me intimately."

ROCKALDA: "Listen – and I will reveal all! I have brought you here to murder you. Tremble for your last hour has come!"

HERBERT: So she seizes him by the throat. But as she raises her arm to strike a ray of moonlight falls on his face.

(A HARP ARPEGGIO MEANS THE MOONLIGHT)

ROCKALDA: (SOFTLY) Oh, I'm enjoying this! (ALOUD) "Merciful heavens, now lovely you are!"

HERBERT: "Strike, woman, effect your evil purpose. I am a Sunday school teacher or else I would resist."

ROCKALDA: "Resistance is useless. Feel that arm!"

HERBERT:	<u>(VERY EXCITED)</u> "The muscles are of steel."
ROCKALDA:	"Exactly. Listen! I am here to kill you but I have seen your face and I love you! Marry me – and your life is spared!"
HERBERT:	"No, no!" <u>(SOFTLY)</u> Do go on, please, this is heaven!
ROCKALDA:	"If you refuse me then beware!"
HERBERT:	"What do you mean?"
ROCKALDA:	"I will toss your body into the middle of yonder lime kiln – and every trace of you will be consumed!"
	<u>(INCREASE BUBBLING EFFECTS)</u>
HERBERT:	<u>(QUIETLY)</u> My God, you're wonderful! <u>(ALOUD)</u> "Marry you? Never! Strike – for my hour is come!"
	<u>(THE SOUNDS ALL CUT SUDDENLY)</u>
ROCKALDA:	Where is he?
HERBERT:	Where's Gripper?
ROCKALDA:	We need Gripper, the detective, to stop me killing my beloved.

HERBERT: He should have been here before this.

(THE SOUND OF A GALLOPING HORSE)

FUDGE: Of course, the last essential character! Surely this is the end of this nightmare.

GILBERT: (V.O.) Mr Fudge could but hope as galloping across a convenient wild cactus-filled prairie close to the Surrey borders came Gripper the detective. Dressed, of course, as a cowboy.

(THE GALLOPING COMES TO A HALT.)

ROCKALDA: Gripper! At last!

HERBERT: You're late!

GRIPPER: (TO HORSE) Whoa, boy, whoa! (TO OTHERS) Of course, I'm late. Sensation detectives are always late. It's obvious why. If he ever stopped being too late then the novel would grind to a halt long before its time. If I bring the villains to justice at the end of volume one, what's to stop the virtuous governess marrying the good young curate at once?

HERBERT: Well, I suppose we should be grateful.

RUTHVEN: Yes, the longer you delay the catastrophe the better.

ALICE: But I must ask – why are you dressed like that?

GRIPPER: It's a disguise. <u>(TO HORSE)</u> Whoa, boy, whoa!

ALICE: Well, it's absurd, quite absurd but I'm not going to grumble so long as I can continue to be persecuted by the infamous Sir Ruthven.

ROCKALDA: We'll all agree with sentiments like that.

GRIPPER: Then I shall take that as an invitation to go on being late. And to assume such preposterous disguises that I shall never contrive to bring anyone to justice.

ALICE: Of course, dear Ruthven, there is still hope. Maybe this time the author intends us for each other. The virtuous young woman has so often been married to the good young man that the reading public must begin to tire of the incessant repetition.

RUTHVEN: No, I'm sorry, but I'm simply too wicked. You'll have to marry the Curate and live happily ever after.

ALICE: Marry and live happily ever after! And this is a novel that pretends to give a picture of life as it is.

ROCKALDA: I mean, if you were to reform Ruthven and Herbert were to

HERBERT:	reform me then all your goodness might actually be of some use.
	Not much hope of reforming you, my love. You don't feel it coming on, do you?
ROCKALDA:	Not a bit – I'm worse than ever.
GRIPPER:	Well, there are still two volumes to go and who knows what may happen.
RUTHVEN:	The usual predictable nonsense.
ALICE;	Why does the public put up with this drivel.

(THE OTHERS AGREE. THEY'RE CUT OFF AS:)

FUDGE: (SUDDENLY LOUD) Excuse me, that is quite enough from you! I'm starting the second volume – right now.

(AS HE STARTS TO WRITE, HE MUTTERS:)

FUDGE: Characters criticising their author – the very idea! They'll be off in search of a new one next! Now – let me see – Volume Two – Chapter the First –

(HE YAWNS AND THEN STARTS TO FALL ASLEEP)

GILBERT: (V.O.) But somehow Mr Fudge fell into a deep sleep only to be woken by a loud bell.

	(A LOUD BELL RINGING)
FUDGE:	(SUDDENLY AWAKE) What?
GILBERT:	(V.O.) He looked about him and realised the scene before his desk was the Round Tower of Windsor Castle. As he watched the characters reassemble, he knew that with or without his help the end of the second volume had been reached.
	(ECHOING CASTLE INTERIOR)
ROCKALDA:	(SIGHS) Ah me!
RUTHVEN:	What's the matter, Rockalda?
ROCKALDA:	Herbert was sent off at the beginning of the second volume as a missionary to Central Africa and he hasn't returned yet. And here we are, for some stupid authorial reason, stuck in Windsor Palace.
HERBERT:	(ENTERING) My Rockalda! At last we meet!
	(THEY KISS)
ROCKALDA:	Tell me when – oh when – do you return from Central Africa?
HERBERT:	Not for several chapters.
ROCKALDA:	That is hard. I don't like this novel at all.
HERBERT:	It's shameful! The publisher told the author that I was getting so confoundedly insipid that no

	reader could stand me so I was sent off to Central Africa for seven years and I'm very much afraid I shall not return till the last chapter. Is Alice all right?
RUTHVEN:	Lovely than ever!
HERBERT:	But you haven't carried her off and married her.
RUTHVEN:	I did try.
ROCKALDA:	And I helped him.
HERBERT:	So what happened? I've been out of the volume altogether, remember.
ROCKALDA:	It happened like this –

(SWITCH TO THE RATTLE OF AN EXPRESS TRAIN)

FUDGE:	Oh no!
GILBERT:	(V.O.) By this point Ebenezer Fudge realised he was hopeless. Events were well and truly out of his control.

(EXPRESS TRAIN CONTINUES)

RUTHVEN:	Alice, of course, was supposed to be travelling by train to Liverpool to join you. But she didn't make it.
HERBERT:	Thank God.
RUTHVEN:	I prevented her. By slaying the pointsman at Rugby Junction and turning the train on to the Midland line.
ROCKALDA:	Then after the train has been turned I crept cautiously along

	the carriages as we entered the tunnel, strangled the engine driver, dressed myself in his clothes – and drove the train safely to Leeds.
	(SOUNDS OF STEAM TRAIN ARRIVING IN STATION)
HERBERT:	So what happened then?
ROCKALDA:	On arriving at Leeds with a ticket clearly stating Liverpool, Alice was brought face to face with the station-master who turned out to be – her father, the Duke of Ben-Nevis who for purposes of his own, had quitted his own lofty station for a station of a totally different description.
HERBERT:	And he recognised her?
ROCKALDA:	He did.
	(CUT TRAIN STATION EFFECTS)
HERBERT:	But – just a moment – aren't you supposed to be the daughter of the Duke of Ben-Nevis?
ROCKALDA:	Yes, but, of course, I'm not. It's the usual story. I turn out to be an imposter and the daughter of a bus-conductor. The complications are too tedious to go into here.

RUTHVEN:	Yes, but it gets worse. I'm afraid that Alice is not the Duke's daughter after all. A fearful presentiment suggests to me that the lovely Alice whom I worship with a devotion absolutely unparalleled is by some ludicrous turn of the plot going to turn out to be –
ALICE:	(ENTERING) Your grand-daughter.
HERBERT:	Alice, this is absurd, even by the standards of these things.
ALICE:	I agree! And why on earth are we meeting in the Round Tower in Windsor Castle –

(THE BELL RINGS AGAIN)

ALICE:	With that terrible bell?
RUTHVEN:	Who knows? But then our author is well known for lazily dropping clues all over the place and then not picking them up.
FUDGE:	I protest! I protest!
GILBERT:	(V.O.) But Mr Fudge was wasting his time. The characters completely ignored him.
RUTHVEN:	All we can be sure of at the end of volume two, Alice, is that you are the daughter of the Duke of Ben-Nevis and he's recognised you.

ALICE:	That's more like it. I'm bored with being an obscure and penniless governess.
ROCKALDA:	But you'll only get recognised as his daughter –
RUTHVEN:	Or possibly my granddaughter –
ROCKALDA:	At the end of the novel.
ALICE:	Yes and in the meantime you have all the fun as Lady Rockalda, murdering people and flashing your mane of blond hair. Even if part of it does turn out to be a wig. I insist on becoming a titled lady at once
ROCKALDA:	Ruthven, we should never have told her all this. It's against all the rules.
ALICE:	I want my jewels now!
HERBERT:	Alice, this is not becoming in a respectable heroine.
ALICE:	I don't care. I'm fed up.
HERBERT:	Only one thing can save us now

(THE BELL STARTS RINGING WILDLY)

ROCKALDA:	Somebody's clambering down the bell rope!
RUTHVEN:	Why – it's Gripper.

(FEET LANDING ON FLOOR AS RINGING STOPS)

GRIPPER:	Who else?

ALICE: But why are you dressed as a Native American?
GRIPPER: You haven't been paying attention to the plot have you? I crept up behind Sir Ruthven as he was switching the points at Rugby and felled him with my tomahawk.
ALICE: Too late to stop him switching the points, of course?
GRIPPER: Of course. And I'm disguised as a Native American because – well, I suppose because I need the tomahawk. By the way, I hope I didn't hurt you too much, Sir Ruthven.
RUTHVEN: No, no, I'm right as rain. I always have prodigious powers of recovery until the last chapter of the book.
GRIPPER: And, of course, once again, I've prevented Alice from getting to Liverpool and sailing to Australia with Herbert and getting marriage on the voyage. If that had happened, where would you all have been?
RUTHVEN: My benefactor!
ALICE: My preserver!
ROCKALDA: My best friend!
HERBERT: My truest ally!
RUTHVEN: Gripper, there is one thing. I've some reason to fear that my darling Alice is going to turn out to be my grand-daughter!
GRIPPER: Well, if you ask my opinion, I fancy not. Indeed – (RUSTLE OF PAPER) I have studied the manuscript of the novel so far

	with some care and I – I have some reason to believe that I am she!
ALL:	You?
GRIPPER:	Ridiculous, isn't it? But listen – <u>(RUSTLE OF PAPER AS READS)</u> "Gripper, the most celebrated detective in the Metropolitan force, was at the same time its youngest member. Although of commanding stature, his face was extremely fair and his features delicately chiselled. His hands were as soft as down, his figure was slight, indeed, almost girlish, and his voice had touching accent in it that was invaluable to him in his assumption of female characters…" <u>(PAUSE)</u> That looks like it, doesn't it?
RUTHVEN:	Yes, yes, my dear long-lost-grand-daughter!
GRIPPER:	Grandfather!
	<u>(THEY EMBRACE. CROSSFADE TO FUDGE SCREAMING AS IF IN HIS SLEEP.)</u>
FUDGE:	Stop! Stop! No… no… this is too much. This can't be happening. I know my plots can be a bit contrived but this… this is madness!
GILBERT:	<u>(V.O.)</u> Suddenly there was quiet. Mr Fudge fell once again into a gin-sodden half-sleep. He

	may or may not have been planning volume three.
	(TOSSING AND TURNING, SNORING)
GILBERT:	(V.O.) But Mr Fudge was all too well acquainted with the experiences of his fellow Ebenezer – Mr Scrooge – and so he knew that the rule of three was bound to apply.
	(SUDDEN THUNDERSTORM)
FUDGE:	Ahhh!
GILBERT:	(V.O.) Mr Fudge was awakened by the sound of a tropical rainstorm. The scene before him was a hut upon a Pacific Island and there dressed in highly decorous versions of supposedly native garb were Herbert the curate and Alice the governess. He knew now he had no choice but to suffer in silence.
	(THE THUNDERSTORM OUTSIDE NOW ABATES)
ALICE:	It's infamous!

HERBERT: It's disgraceful!

ALICE: Here we are just before the last chapter and I'm about to be married to the man I abominate!

HERBERT: And I to the woman I detest!

ALICE: Oh, I'll give you such a time when we're married!

HERBERT: And I'll do the same. Then we can get divorced.

ALICE: So how exactly did you get from Central Africa to Algiers to here?

HERBERT: Didn't you read chapter four? I walked – I swam – and bound palm tree branches together and canoed – and here I am. How about you?

ALICE: Well, after I was recognised by my father, the Duke of Ben-Nevis –

HERBERT: Who presumably gave up ticket-collecting at Leeds Station?

ALICE: Oh yes, indeed declared it was impossible for me to marry someone as lowly as a Sunday school teacher. For a time I was happy because I thought I might be intended for the evil Sir Ruthven after all. But, no, the irritating author would not here of it and shipped me out here to be a missionary.

HERBERT: But what has become of the disgraced ex-Lady Rockalda?

ROCKALDA:	(ENTERING) I am here!
GILBERT:	(V.O.) And as if things weren't absurd enough here was the fair-haired panther-like seductress wearing a pearl necklace and seventeen palm leaves.
HERBERT:	Rockalda! My love!

(THEY EMBRACE)

HERBERT:	So – why have you been brought out here?
ROCKALDA:	(WEARILY) I expect I am to turn up at your wedding. I rather think that – stricken with remorse – I worked my passage out here as a stewardess that I might stagger into the church as you are being united and tell you that you are no other than Sir Ruthven Glenaloon.
HERBERT:	Oh no! And let me guess – he who has hitherto passed as that baronet is only a bus-conductor.
ROCKALDA:	Something like that.
HERBERT: Alice.	Here's a blow to your hopes,
ALICE:	Not at all. Baronet or busman, I adore him and when you and I are divorced he shall be mine. (PAUSE) By the way, where is he?

ROCKALDA:	I don't know. We're supposed to all meet here before the last chapter. (RUSTLE OF PAPER) We've got the heading and that's all.
HERBERT:	I hope nothing has happened to him.
ALICE:	Happened to him! Don't say he's dead!
ROCKALDA:	I sincerely hope not! Are you in the chapter that's just been written?
ALICE:	No.
ROCKALDA:	Nor you?
HERBERT:	No!
ROCKALDA:	Well, we'd better see what it's all about –
	(RUSTLE OF PAPER.)
	(CROSSFADE TO SEPULCHRAL TICKING CLOCK)
ROCKALDA:	(READING) "Sir Ruthven stood alone in the sepulchral family hall of the family castle which he knew now beyond all doubt was not his by right. In his hand he carried a hatchet…"
RUTHVEN:	(IN THE SCENE) "Now to end a life that has long been too burdensome to bear…"

ROCKALDA: (READING) "He swung the ponderous axe three times round his head and towards the middle of the third swing the blade shot like lightning through the thickest part of the bad man's neck!

(A SCREECH FROM RUTHVEN)

ROCKALDA: (READING) "The head bounded into the air and fell heavily on the stone floor."

(HEAD HITS FLOOR)

ROCKALDA: (READING) "The lips still moved spasmodically. With a frightful effort, they managed to hiss –"

RUTHVEN: (CROAKILY) "A very neat blow…"

(PAUSE)

HERBERT: Poor old Ruthven, he was a good fellow out of the novel.

ALICE: But this is intolerable! I love that man! And this time the author's chosen to behead him

	in the most gruesome way. Isn't it about time we demanded the novel ended as we like?
HERBERT:	I agree. But what can we do?
ROCKALDA:	Summon the author! His ridiculous plots have ruled our lives too long!

(THE OTHERS AGREE. THE RUDDIGORE GHOST MUSIC RETURNS.)

FUDGE:	(IN HIS SLEEP) No! No! No!
GILBERT:	(V.O.) And in his gin-fuelled stupor, Mr Fudge found himself summoned before his own characters.
ALICE:	You have killed off Sir Ruthven!
FUDGE:	But he was a black-hearted villain! You don't want him back, do you?
HERBERT:	Of course.
FUDGE:	But you're the hero!
HERBERT:	I object to him being slaughtered on my account!
ROCKALDA:	Restore him to life at once!
FUDGE:	Now, you Rockalda, I can understand. You miss the evil abettor of all your schemes and –

ALICE:	Give me back my love!
FUDGE:	But you're the quiet, virtuous heroine!
ALICE:	Have you learned nothing?
FUDGE:	But don't you want to marry Herbert? He comes into a baronetcy in the last chapter!
ALICE:	I don't care! I hate mild and amiable men! I like handsome rogues who set all laws at defiance. Do you understand? I don't want to marry an insipid Sunday School teacher! I want to marry the deliciously, seductively evil Sir Ruthven!
FUDGE:	But it's already been written. He chops his head off.
ALICE:	Science can do anything. Invent a process if you have it not.
	<u>(GHOSTLY MUSIC AND GHOSTLY FOOTSTEPS)</u>
FUDGE:	Ahhhhh!!!!
GILBERT:	<u>(V.O.)</u> And then to Ebenezer Fudge's dismay, Sir Ruthven appeared – with his head tucked underneath his arm.
RUTHVEN:	<u>(SOFTLY)</u> Do as we ask!
FUDGE:	<u>(PANICKING)</u> Oh very well – very well – I can't stand any more. Alice – you want me to

	put his head back on so you can marry him?
ALICE:	Of course!
FUDGE:	And – Herbert – you want to marry the Lady Rockalda - this yellow-haired fiend with panther-like movements and –
HERBERT:	Certainly!
FUDGE:	So will you reform her?
HERBERT:	Does it really matter?
RUTHVEN:	(DARKLY) If you don't put my head back on my shoulders I am going to wave it about. We might even play football with it!

(THE OTHERS AGREE)

FUDGE:	Very well, very well, I agree. But what about –
THE OTHERS:	Gripper?

(A BICYCLE BELL)

GILBERT:	(V.O.) At this point in the nightmare, Gripper the sensation detective, entered the hut dressed as a Yeoman of the Guard on a bicycle equipped with bladders to support it through high seas. It was the final straw.

GRIPPER:	But what about me?
FUDGE:	You're too late!
GRIPPER:	That isn't my fault.
FUDGE:	Well, I have a surprise for you. At the end of the novel you turn out to be –
GRIPPER:	Sir Ruthven's abandoned granddaughter! My instinct was right! And I – I don't like it.
FUDGE:	You'll be a very fine woman!
GRIPPER:	I'd rather be a fine man!
FUDGE:	You're going to marry an earl!
GRIPPER:	I'd prefer a countess!
FUDGE:	Can we leave it doubtful?
GRIPPER:	On no account. If you don't give me a sensible plot resolution then I'll never work for you again. I'm a sensation detective. You can't get on without any of us!
ROCKALDA:	We are your stock characters!
RUTHVEN:	You can't manage without us!
HERBERT:	Your career as a writer will be finished!
ALICE:	We deserve better!

(THE VOICES OVERLAP)

(CROSSFADE TO A FEVERISH FUDGE)

FUDGE: Very well, very well, I give in. I'll alter the last chapter. Herbert shall marry Rockalda. Ruthven shall be restored to life and marry Alice. And – and Gripper shall turn out to be Sherlock Holmes in disguise. There! What do you say to that?

GILBERT: (V.O.) What the causes of this extraordinary phantasmogorical experience were, Ebenezer Fudge never knew. Gin? Overwork? Lack of sleep? What he decided to do was write up the events of the night under the title of A Sensation Novel. The book was regarded as groundbreaking and strikingly original in its challenge to the tired conventions of the genre. So, of course, the book sold very, very badly.

(PLAYOUT MUSIC AND CREDITS)

THE END

www.ingramcontent.com/pod-product-compliance
Ingram Content Group UK Ltd.
Pitfield, Milton Keynes, MK11 3LW, UK
UKHW041257180426
11947UKWH00008B/530